CANNON FODDER

OR THE SECRET LIVES OF HENCHMEN

A NOVEL

KYLE DECKER

Copyright © 2012, 2014 by Kyle Decker.

Published by Rogue's Gallery Publishers.

First Revised Edition.

Cover and book design by Kevin Fitzgerald.
Author photo courtesy of Amanda Clifford.

ISBN 978-0-9886698-1-9 (paperback)

CANNON FODDER

OR THE SECRET LIVES OF HENCHMEN

For Ma.

"Elkhart Global Dynamics strives to achieve the boundless possibilities. Our innovations push the world forward and it is our goal to provide a guiding hand to all of the world's people. We are dedicated in our mission to lead the way towards a better tomorrow. Elkhart Global Dynamics is a company with its eyes to the bright future and its hands always working to build it."
–Elkhart Global Dynamics mission statement

1/ THE SECRET AGENT

"Wise men never care to hear the odds."
–Damien Elkhart

Ian Fleming was right. The scent and smoke and sweat of a casino are nauseating at three in the morning, and trying to pick out the tuxedo-clad secret agent from England among the tuxedo-clad accountants from the north side of Chicago strains the eyes, especially after eight hours.

Number 21 could barely even blink without a terrible scratching sensation on his dried eyes. He forced a yawn to try and drum up some moisture, but to no avail. He looked around to see if any of the other henchmen were about, trying to gauge their levels of comfort and weigh them against his own. Where was the agent? They had intelligence that MI6 agent Liam Adams was in this casino. If he was, 21 sure as hell hadn't seen him. He felt as if some unseen force was squeezing on his heart like a rubber stress ball. This Liam Adams had been a thorn in Mr. Elkhart's side for years.

Adams's motives for digging into Elkhart Global Dynamics' goals were a non-issue for 21. As far as he was concerned, all that mattered was Adams had put his job in jeopardy. Number 21 had just been promoted and he wanted to justify his advance from a mere security guard to the goon squad.

He'd certainly put in the time. He always showed up early and stood by the punch clock, waiting to punch in. Painted on the wall above the clock was the motivational slogan "Excellence WILL Be Tolerated." The punch clock was programmed to keep people from punching in too early. When his supervisor passed he seemed happy to see 21 had been early again.

His mind was tired of scanning, and so it wandered back two weeks to when he had gotten the promotion. He'd been guarding the north perimeter. He'd just been lucky. He stopped to pee and he saw it. A manhole cover popped open in one of the empty water retention areas.

A man, in what looked a lot like a scuba suit, popped out. Had Number 21 kept going on the usual rotation and not stopped briefly for a piss, he would never have seen him. As it would happen, the man had been spending a good deal of time monitoring the guard movements and had tried to time this out perfectly; he just didn't factor in the very important variable of the two cans of soda Number 21 drank prior to his shift. As 21 had been instructed, he asked no questions, did not pause. He did not look at the man or even think about it. He just fired. His first shot pierced the neck. The man fell coughing. 21 used the scope to put three more shots in the man's head. And that was that.

He'd received a large pay bump as a result. He also made love to his wife Mary that night, who was so happy with him she was particularly wild. They'd left their two children with the neighbors and they made all the noise they damn well pleased.

21 got slightly hard from this memory but quickly tried to take his mind off it so as not to embarrass himself. He adjusted his pants so his penis didn't press up against his concealed gun. It was then that he spotted Liam Adams sitting at a high stakes poker table. The game had grown intense and a crowd had formed to watch. 21 blended into the observing crowd and made eye contact with the other henchmen. From his vantage point he could see Adams was doing well. The only other remaining player was a surly looking Middle Eastern man.

Number 21 recognized the man from the briefing as Raees, a major shareholder in an oil company with whom Elkhart Global Dynamics did business. Seeing Adams at a poker table with Raees meant he was definitely on to something. Number 21 wasn't close enough to hear what was being said, but the body language suggested the usual contest of wills such scenes often represent. Suddenly Raees stood up, trying to hide his belligerence in an attempt to save his remaining pride. Adams smiled at something Raees said. As Raees exited, Adams stood up, refastened his cuff links and tipped the cashier.

It was time to make their move, grab Adams, and find out what he knew. Adams brushed right past 21.

"Beg your pardon," Adams said with a cool stare, looking 21 in the eye.

"Quite alright," was all 21 could manage. As Adams continued on, 21 followed in pursuit. The other henchmen, keen to what was happening, began to move as well. Number 21 was the first into the main lobby, but Adams was nowhere to be found. The sound of a closing door caught Number 21's attention. He turned and saw the source: an access door to the stairwell. 21's two comrades caught up with him and he signaled to the door. The others drew their concealed weapons as Number 21 opened the stairwell. They moved inside and waited for the door to close. Number 21 drew his gun and signaled for one to wait by the door and the other to follow. Mary would be so proud of the initiative he was showing. He hoped his bosses would be as well.

From the bottom of the stairs he heard a sneeze, followed shortly by another sneeze. Before he could turn he felt a silencer pressed into the lower back of his head. He didn't hear anything.

Three jobs became available.

2/ ORIENTATION DAY

"One can exist, but they are not truly born until they follow Truth."
—Damien Elkhart

DYLAN: #23

Dylan Roffredo stood in line on orientation day. He fidgeted a great deal, as he often did in situations where he felt awkward. He'd been standing in line for a solid thirty-five minutes among a group of men who were all staring straight forward. Dylan was a talkative young man and as such the instructions not to speak left him feeling very much out of place. Dylan had applied for an internship at Elkhart Global Dynamics, a weapons manufacturer as well as one of the world's largest defense contractors. The company's clients included some of the most powerful countries in the world. Elkhart Global Dynamics's internship program was highly regarded, promising as much as a year's worth of college credit for less than four months of work. Dylan took a few breaths from his inhaler. Anxiety always made his asthma act up.

When he was next in line, Dylan cleared his throat and shifted through his papers, making sure that everything was in order. He tapped the bottom and sides of the paper against the flat surface of the wall. When he was satisfied that the pages were straight and in order, he once again commenced fidgeting.

The door buzzed and he entered the office. It was small and most of the space was taken up by the large metal desk. There were no windows; aeration was permitted only by a small vent in the upper right corner of the wall behind the desk. Some string tied to the vent waved and a small water stain on the wall suggested that perhaps a pipe had burst at some point in the past. There was a poster of half a glass of water on the wall with the caption "Either Way Only You Can Fill It!"

The man behind the desk asked for Dylan's papers, never looking away from his computer, which appeared two or three years out of date. With a pathetic attempt at confidence in his voice, Dylan reached out his hand and said, "Hi, I'm..."

"No names," the man said. His hair was dark and oily. It was slicked to the side and he wore a protector in the pocket of his short-sleeved collared shirt. The oily-haired, pocket-protector man had no nameplate on his desk, just a number. 11. It was then that Dylan remembered the ad for the job had mentioned no names were used. He felt his face flush ever so slightly.

11 took a stamp, adjusted one number on the bottom, and pounded it one time onto an ink pad and three times on Dylan's files. He entered data into the computer at a speed Dylan had to admire. 11 put one paper into an old filing cabinet and the other through a paper shredder below the desk.

Just as Dylan was about to sit in the folding chair in the corner, the man quickly handed him a sheet of paper and said, "23."

Dylan took the sheet of paper.

"Don't forget that number," 11 said.

"23," said Dylan.

"While you're here, this is what you will go by. It is how you will be addressed. It is how you will introduce yourself. Elkhart Global asks that all employees go only by their numbers. If you give your real name to anybody, you will be terminated. Do you understand?"

"Yes," said 23. "I certainly don't want to be fired."

"Take these papers and head down the hall, take a left. Room Four," 11 said.

23 took the papers and headed down the hall. He turned right. He noticed the room numbers were going the wrong way. He corrected himself, turned around, and quietly hoped that nobody had noticed.

Room Four was considerably nicer than 11's office. The room was decorated with various company slogans and motivational posters. A woman with a tight-fitting lab coat took one of 23's papers. She wrote something on it, handed it back to him, scratched something off on her clipboard, and told him to have a seat at the numbered desk. A quick glance at her breasts revealed a tag by her collar, Number 9. Her dark hair was pulled back into a ponytail. She had thick-framed black glasses, full lips, and a beauty mark just above them and slightly to the right. Number 23 smiled slightly but she didn't see.

At the desk 23 found a name tag with his number and a packet of information. Number 23 glanced around at the others sitting around the room. He tried to determine if he should put on his name tag now and open the pack or if he should wait until further instructions. He decided on the latter. He folded his hands and just looked forward. He resisted the urge to fidget. He focused his attention to a poster featuring a soldier in a uniform he did not recognize. The equipment looked very futuristic, as if out of a science fiction movie. The poster read: "Elkhart Global Dynamics: The Future of Tomorrow!"

After about ten minutes, five more people had entered the room. Number 9 scratched on her clipboard and then closed the door. She locked it by entering a code on a keypad and then took center stage in the room.

"Good morning. Welcome to Elkhart Global Dynamics. We look forward to working with all of you. Please save any questions until the end of the presentation. From here on out, you will only be referred to by your assigned number. Use of birth names is grounds for immediate termination. No exceptions." Number 9 waited a brief moment for this to sink in. "It should also be noted that your assigned number is the number you will carry with you for your entire time here at Elkhart Global. This number has nothing to do with your rank, or the order in which you were employed. It is randomly assigned. There will be no trading of numbers. Please place your tags on now if you have not already."

23 had not yet placed on his tag and, as per instructions, took the opportunity to do so.

"Open your information packets to page one."

Welcome to the Elkhart team!
Elkhart Global Dynamics is a non-union company. We offer an extensive benefits package including full dental, health and life insurance policies, as well as a 401(k) and profit sharing. In other words, when the company does well, you do well.

9 then instructed the group to fill out various forms, which included their insurance and benefits information. She also mentioned that for

those who wished to get college credit, an additional form could be found on page seven and also filled out at that time. Number 23 did so.

"If everyone's ready," the shapely Number 9 said, "Please turn to page 10. The following is very important. So pay attention." Number 9 read this page out loud in a no-nonsense tone that intimidated Number 23.

Elkhart Global Dynamics is a very essential company in the progress of mankind. As a result, Elkhart Global Dynamics takes a very serious stand on the standards and practices of all of its employees. The following are grounds for IMMEDIATE TERMINATION. No exceptions.

Use of birth names.
Failure to carry out a direct order from a superior.
Leaking any information to anyone outside of the company.
Use of alcohol or illicit drugs while on company time.
Arriving for your shift under the influence of alcohol or illicit drugs.
Allowing non-employees on the premises at any time.
Having sexual liaisons with fellow employees.
Causing the failure of a project.
Discussion of lives outside on company time.
Failure to report or immediately eliminate any trespassers on the premises.
Going Absent Without Leave (AWOL).
Stealing from E.G.D.

At the bottom of the list was a line to confirm one's agreement with a signature. Considering failure to agree would result in not getting the job, 23 signed it, as did everyone else in the room.

"Now," said Number 9, "we will view the company's introductory video. Please remain seated and silent until the end."

A screen lowered from the ceiling in the front of the room. The lights dimmed and the projector hanging from the back of the room clicked on, producing a yellow triangle of illumination. The dust floating in the light stole Number 23's attention briefly from the screen.

Number 23 thought: "This is where I will make my impact."

TYLER: #12

After college, Tyler Kelly (or T.K., as he was referred to by his mother and closest friends) found himself about seventy grand in debt to his student loan company. Upon hearing about what Elkhart Global Dynamics offered at a career fair, T.K. decided to go work for them. He was assigned the Number 12 and pointed in the direction of Room Four.

Outside the room was an incredibly attractive woman with her hair pulled up, glasses, and movie star breasts. She took his papers, looked them over, stamped them, and handed one back saying, "Welcome to Elkhart Global, Number 12. We hope you enjoy your time here."

"I think I will," Number 12 said, firing off a wink.

She half smiled. He took a seat. But instead of looking at the packet on his desk, 12 continued to look at the woman at the door, who was too busy to take notice. She was definitely now in the spank-bank.

"That's Number 9," said a voice from behind.

12 turned around to see a younger man sitting behind them, "Excuse me?"

"The woman," he said. "Her number is 9. What's yours?"

"It's uh," he looked at his papers, "12."

"I'm 23."

KARL: #17

Karl Jenson only had a GED, but for the purposes of Elkhart Global Dynamics it was more than sufficient. Henching had become one of the fastest growing professions; the company wasn't too picky. Although the risk factors were high, it paid well and all that mattered to Karl was that paycheck and top-notch insurance policy. Karl noticed the bullet holes in the wall as he stood in line. Somebody was once gunned down right where he was standing.

His phone started ringing with a top-forty song. "Yeah?"

"Hey. This is your sister."

"I know, Sarah," Karl said, "Phones these days, they got caller ID."

"Yeah... anyway," she said letting his jibe roll off her back, "how's the new job?"

"I'm still in line at orientation."

"You don't have to do this, you know," Sarah said.

"Well, if you can find a better paying job for people without a college degree, I'd take it."

"I can help too, y'know. I'll stop going to school..."

"No, dammit," he said. "You're staying in school. That's final."

"Fine, Mr. Martyr," she quipped. "I'm sure they'll write songs about you."

"They'd better," he said. "Listen. I have to go. I'll talk to you later."

"Later, bro."

Karl and Sarah's parents had passed away during the holiday break before Karl's last semester of high school. He dropped out to work full time and raise money to pay off various debts left by his parents. His sister Sarah, three years his junior, was a brilliant girl who had been correcting his math homework for him at the age of five. To continue to pay for her college, he needed this job. He pushed the danger to the back of his mind and took his seat in Room Four.

Number 9 stepped forward and gave her presentation. 12 didn't pay attention entirely, just enough to get the gist of it and scope the high-riding skirt on the presenter. She then stepped aside, the lights dimmed, and a short introduction film started up.

On screen a man in a suit walked onto a stage with blue curtains and multi-colored lights.

"Welcome to Elkhart Global Dynamics!" he began, "We're so glad you've made the conscious decision to join us in our mission to bring the world into a new era. You've all shown various characteristics and skills that we believe will benefit the company, the world, and yes, even yourselves. Our mission is simple, but far from easy."

23 feverishly scratched notes into the margins of his information packet.

The image of the company logo was projected on the curtain as the host recited the company's mission statement. "Elkhart Global Dynamics strives to achieve the boundless possibilities. Our innovations push the world forward, and it is our goal to provide a guiding hand to all of the world's people. We are dedicated in our mission to lead the way toward a better tomorrow. Elkhart Global Dynamics is a company with its eyes facing the bright future and its hands always working to build it." Throughout his speech images flashed of sunsets and landscapes that were somehow considered inspiring, though 12 didn't see how a landscape could be inspiring. When a silhouetted image of two men helping each other climb onto a pile of rocks overlooking a bay appeared, 12 turned to doodling in the corners of his info packet. Mostly eyes. He always doodled eyes.

"It's difficult work. But we have the resources," images jumped from machinery, to oil fields, to labs, "we have the ambition, and we have you," and finally to images of workers in order to really emphasize that the company included its workers among its assets. "We remind you again of the high risk factor of the work you will be doing. Those of you without military or mercenary background will be trained accordingly depending on your various positions. But there will be more on that later."

12 doodled 9 in a sexy pose with a word balloon, "More on this later."

Part 1: Company History

"Elkhart Global Dynamics started with one man and a dream." During the voiceover a portrait of Damien Elkhart was shown. He was tall and handsome, with a well-groomed circle beard and a scar peeking out from behind an eyepatch over his right eye. He was sitting in a chair in front of a fireplace.

"Damien Elkhart. Mr. Elkhart saw the world for the chaos that it was. He knew he could do much better and improve the world. Mr. Elkhart built a company from the ground up. Through this he hoped to gain the resources to raise the money and power to unite the world's people."

17 watched in silence. He jotted no notes and made no doodles. He heard the information, but none of it stuck. His mind was more on the delayed paycheck. He saw the black-and-white image of a man in a lab coat and cumbersome safety goggles, he heard the narration, but it eventually became white noise to his mental montage of unpaid bills and next semester's tuition for Sarah.

"Having studied rocket science, Mr. Elkhart built an empire up from the ground by manufacturing weapons. Elkhart Global Dynamics was born." A swelling soundtrack of mighty horns blared as the logo formed on the screen.

"In order to protect his investments, Damien Elkhart bought up a fading private defense firm." The EGD logo fused with another and swelled. "With the combination of Elkhart's advanced weapons and the defense firm's talented mercenaries, Elkhart Global Dynamics built a private militia that rivaled the armies of even the most powerful countries in the world. And it continues to grow to this very day. Elkhart Global Dynamics is more than just a weapons manufacturer and defense contractor. It has built an entire empire of subsidiary companies including oil, banking, shipping, news media, and even insurance to ensure that all of our employees are best covered in the ways they need. Elkhart also owns and operates numerous criminal rehabilitation facilities around the world. Elkhart offers jobs to ex-cons and inmates, helping put an end to recidivism.

"Damien Elkhart continues to mastermind and oversee the company's projects even now."

Part 2: Taking Pride In What You Do

"Now you too are a part of the history of Elkhart Global Dynamics and soon to be part of the history of the world. Elkhart is a company that takes a 'by any means necessary' approach to achieving many of its goals, but we assure you that the ends will justify these means. There are various groups from all walks of life that see it differently, and have made numerous attempts in the past to impede our progress. This is where many of you come in. It will fall on you, no matter what your position, to keep your eyes open for any suspicious activity and react swiftly and accordingly. For this reason you will all be issued firearms and trained how too use them.

"Henching is a job with a long and rich history." Pictures of squires bringing knights weapons and armor enlightened the audience with examples from history, fleshed out with Ken Burns-style zooms and pans. "The word 'henchman' means 'a trusted follower.' That means we trust you. Back in the 1500s the word used was 'minion,' which meant a squire or an apprentice. As with the squires of old, it means you are helping dress Elkhart in armor so that you may learn how to one day wear it yourself. And you will do this by striving to the Elkhart Ideal."

Part 3: A Word from Damien Elkhart

"And now a personal message from Damien Elkhart himself."

Damien Elkhart appeared on screen again, this time as more than a photo.

"Good day, friends, and welcome to the Elkhart family. I wanted to let you all know how much I truly appreciate you becoming a part of my efforts. I think we can all agree the world has fallen into chaos. The world has slipped into darkness, so much so that people can no longer see the Truth that is right in front of them. But I have a vision. It is a vision of Truth. I have seen this light for myself and will do all I can to bring this light to all of the world's people. But I cannot do this alone. For joining me in these efforts, I truly thank you. Together we can unite all of the world's people under this one Truth.

"Thank you for joining us in our efforts to build a better world. And welcome. Welcome to the Elkhart Team!"

Part 4: Dedicating Yourself to Your Job, Dedicating Yourself to Truth

The host of the video emerged wearing what appeared to be a work uniform of sorts.

"We here at Elkhart Global Dynamics believe in the Elkhart Ideal. Namely, that we can make the world a better place. Dedicating yourself to your job means dedicating yourself to this Truth, to this Ideal. And you will help us bring this Truth to the rest of the world."

3/ OSHA: "HERO" PREVENTION

Excerpted from the Elkhart Global Dynamics Employee Manual
presented by the Occupational Safety and Health Administration

*Employees of Elkhart Global Dynamics will commonly experience a
very unique occupational hazard. This is known as the "Hero" Factor.
Due to the controversial nature of Elkhart Global's goals and practices,
the company's facilities are under constant threat of terrorist-like
activities. These misguided groups are numerous and ever-changing.
Once new threats in this area become apparent your supervisor will
call a meeting to brief you on the individual groups and their M.O.s.
Pay attention to the on-site training so that you can learn how best to
protect yourself and the company's assets.*

*Any suspicious activity should be immediately reacted to. Should any
apparent heroes, spies, or saboteurs be discovered, shoot to kill. And
do so immediately. Also be sure to inform any superiors so that other
areas of the facility can be scanned and security codes altered. Just
remember this mnemonic device. S.C.A.M.*

S. Shoot to Kill
C. Confirm the Kill
A. Alert a Superior
M. Maintain Your Position

*Heroes are often highly skilled in various forms of combat. In
some cases they can even possess what may seem like superhuman
abilities. Some may be skilled in stealth, others in gun play, others
are very adept at martial arts and Close Quarters Combat. You will
be trained in basic C.Q.C.; however, when encountering a "Hero,"
the key is numbers. Very few employees stand a chance in one-on-
one encounters with these so-called "Heroes." So remember, alert
surrounding comrades and outnumber, surround, and overwhelm.*

Maintaining calm is key.

Do not rush in one at a time. Surround. Outnumber. Overwhelm.

And again, be sure to maintain your calm. During battle, panic can set in on everyone. Seeing numerous co-workers fall at the hands of one or two individuals is, indeed, a nerve-racking sight. The following mnemonic device will be your Best Friend Forever:

B. Breathe
F. Focus
F. Fight

Calm and focus are the keys to keeping your head about you in battle. Lose your calm, and you might lose your life.

This has been OSHA: "Hero" Prevention Training, exclusive for Elkhart Global Dynamics. Stay alive.

4/ KENNY D

"Everyone has a talent. It is just useless until guided with the right hands."
–Damien Elkhart

At twenty-five Ken was in prison for a second time. Ken had been running with The Dukes since his cousin had introduced him. He started as a lookout, but he quickly moved up to mule. He would often be asked to smuggle drugs inside various toys, which would then be opened upon arrival to the destination. His first trip to Juvy was for assault after an altercation with a rival gang who had been caught dealing in The Dukes territory. The cops showed up. Everyone split. Some got caught. Kenny D was one of them, simple as that.

Since then Kenny had climbed the ladder a great deal. His ability to think fast had eventually earned him a position of a general of sorts in The Dukes, planning out various "jobs" and fights. Kenny was doing time for a liquor store robbery he had planned. An off-duty police officer was the only snafu.

When the guards came to take him, there was a woman with them. She had very nice tits. Her name tag merely had the number 9 on it. She smiled at him.

"Greetings," she said. "We have an offer for you." She handed him a card. Kenny took it.

He filled out the forms to get his possessions back. He turned around and the door buzzed.

"I'll take it from here," she said to the guards. The guards only nodded.

"So what the fuck is this?" Kenny asked, looking at the card which read:

Elkhart Global Dynamics

"Taking the World Forward"

"I represent Elkhart Global Dynamics. We're one of the largest defense contractors and weapons manufacturers in the world. We're looking for strong, enthusiastic young men to work for us."

"You want to hire me? I have a record." Kenny paused. "You just picked me up from fuckin' county."

"It's actually because of your history, especially your activities with The Dukes, that we feel you fit our profile." She unlocked her car, which chirped with a "whoop whoop." It was a sleek black Ferrari. "Get in."

"This your car?"

"Only the finest at Elkhart." she said.

Kenny did as he was told, and they were off.

"What profile do I fit, exactly?" Kenny inquired.

"We need people who are able and willing to perform certain actions that will assist in the completion of our various projects. Based on your position in your street gang we see you have some potential to work for us on some of these jobs."

Kenny understood what she was getting at and smiled. "What's in it for me?" Kenny needed to know.

"Our company pulls in more each financial quarter than the gross national product of most countries," she explained. "Now. Are you interested?"

"Yeah," Kenny said, "I'm down."

She handed him a folder.

"We've taken the liberty of filling out your application for you. We just need you to verify your information."

Kenny didn't question how this woman or her company had access to his information. But it was all correct and he signed it.

"Welcome to the Elkhart team, Number 45."

5/ BIRTH OF A FEMME FATALE

"Damaged people can be rebuilt only if one is forceful enough."
–Damien Elkhart

She was called Lucy when she was taken in by child services. She was living with her father and brother. Her mother had died in childbirth. When Lucy was seven years old, her brother put his fingers inside of her. After that she did not speak to the other children in the neighborhood. Her brother would get strung out and feel her up at least once a month. It took her two years to finally tell her father. Once her father found out about these goings-on, he tried to pimp her out for drug money. For fifty dollars he'd put her in a room with a man for twenty five minutes. But one time before she was thrown into her bedroom she stole a steak knife from the kitchen. The man smiled at her and told her to sit on his lap. She did as she was told, and she could feel his penis getting hard inside his sweat pants. He began to slide his hand up her dress. She did not cry. She only drew the knife and thrust it into the man's leg. He sat up quickly.

"Jesus Fuck!" He proclaimed, "Ugh! You little... fucking... twat!" he shrieked.

Her father came in the door after hearing the commotion. The other man struck him, "What's your game, cocksucker?! You trying to kill me, take my money?" The two men began to fight and yell and curse. Lucy's father drew a gun and shot the other man. Lucy hid in the closet. The neighbors had called the police, who took Lucy's father away when they arrived. Lucy was taken in by child services.

She was sitting alone in the corner one day when a man came into the orphanage. He was handsome and had an eyepatch. All the other children saw him and giggled. They thought he was a pirate. He looked over them and observed them for a good long while. Occasionally he'd point to one and ask the social services people questions. They would shuffle through the files and give what answers they could. Eventually they went into the office. The office had a window so that the workers could see the children, but that time it was the children looking into the office. Lucy still sat in the corner. The man wrote down a number and slid the paper across the table. The people who ran the orphanage saw the number. The lady began to cry and the man smiled. They hugged. Damien Elkhart walked out of the office and over to Lucy. He crouched down in front of her, held out his hand, and said,

"Hello, Lucy. My name is Damien Elkhart. I have heard your story. I have the answers you need. Come with me and I will show you Truth."

Lucy took his hand and became Number 9.

Over the following years Number 9 was trained in just about everything a femme fatale would need to excel in the field, from martial arts to gun play. She was also trained about the inner workings of the company, and was even schooled extensively in Damien Elkhart's visions of Truth.

6/ THE TANK

"The only difference between a hero and a villain is which side you are on."
–Damien Elkhart

Numbers 12 and 17 had been assigned to pull a raid. They were to break into a pharmaceutical company and steal the research that had been done on a mood stabilizer the company had been developing. Once Elkhart Dynamics had this in their possession, they would have enough over the company to consume it entirely. The two young men sat next to each other during the briefing.

"Looks like we'll be working together," Number 17 said.

"Looks like," 12 responded. He stuck out his hand. "I'm Ty-shit. I mean, Number 12."

"Well, 12. They call me 17."

"Enough of the introductions," said the man who appeared to be in charge. "We've got work to do." The man giving the briefing was Number 75. He was a no-nonsense middle-management type.

A layout of the target building was projected onto the screen. "I'm only going to go through this once, so keep your eyes and ears open. The better you pay attention, the better chance you have of getting out of this alive. This should be an easy one anyway.

"Now, the guards rotate their shifts at 2300. That's when we will make our move. Is is during this time we will blow the fence and rush the back docks. At this point our tech guys will already have taken out the alarms. Since we trust our co-workers to do their jobs, we shouldn't have to worry about those.

"Once we get into the center of the lab, we will be taking all the hard copies of the records and transferring all the research data onto an external hard-drive. After that we torch the building and all records and research. We leave them nothing. Then we're the fuck out of Dodge, holding all of the cards worth holding."

"So long as it's not aces and eights," 12 said to 17. 17 chuckled.

"Questions? Comments? Or just smart ass remarks?" Number 75 quipped.

"No. Nothing. Sorry," 12 said.

"Don't apologize to me. It's your own ass you're putting on the line. Guys like you never last," he said.

Number 75 was a hardened veteran and had seen a lot of men come and a lot of men go. He was considerably bitter that he'd been assigned to work with so much new meat. This batch consisted of pussies and smart-asses. This was the group he was to lead into Diamond Pharmaceuticals.

Less than two hours later, Number 75 sat in an old water-retention ditch down the road from the Diamond Pharmaceuticals laboratory. He munched on the end of a burning cigar as he sat in wait for the signal that the alarms had been killed.

"The baby is asleep," his radio informed him.

"Roger that," he replied.

He signaled to the men and checked his watch. It was five minutes till the shift change. He used hand signs to communicate this to the group around him. When the time came he nodded, tossed his cigar, and charged the gate. The group followed. He smashed the face of the gate operator with the butt of his gun and then fired two rounds at the armed guard a few yards away. The man went down. 75 and a select few covered everyone as they entered the building. The first wave through covered the door, while the remaining henchmen entered. A few stayed outside and covered the exits.

Numbers 12 and 17 spread out and began planting the bombs. The bombs stuck to surfaces and could be detonated individually or all at once.

"How we comin' with those remote mines, Smartass?" 75 asked.

"Almost there," said 12.

"Good," 75 shifted his attention to the hacker uploading the data to their external hard-drive. "Alright, Nerd, do your thing."

"Uploading the data now," he said.

"Time?" 75 asked.

"Five minutes."

"Keep on your toes, men," 75 commanded, "Hold for five."

There was a loud explosion and men from outside came pouring in, dead bodies surfing the blast wave.

"Holy living fuck!" exclaimed 75.

Storming in through the door came one of the city's several masked vigilantes. This was The Tank. The Tank was a large, hulking man who wore a suit of armor. He was also a packhorse for weaponry.

The Tank charged through the henchmen covering the interior of the door. A swing of his forearm caved in heads, busted jaws, and shattered torsos. The room filled with a sound not unlike trees being cracked in a storm. The Tank shot off smoke bombs, which due to his visor didn't impair his vision in the way it did everyone else's.

"Pussy ass faggot!" proclaimed 75 as he charged The Tank, unloading an entire clip in the process. Of course The Tank was aptly named, and the barrage of gunfire merely made him stumble back slightly.

75's gun went click, click, click. Taking this opportunity The Tank shot a single round into 75's chest. Even with a flak jacket under his uniform, 75 was split in half. What was left of his body hit the floor and lay there looking like some forgotten ground zero.

Number 12 signaled to Number 17, and Number 17 nodded and signaled back. 17 ran over to the hacker, or what was left of him. The download had completed and he unplugged the laptop and threw it into the knapsack. During this time 12 had taken cover around a corner and shot off a round or two off to draw the attention of The Tank. A dart with a flashing light stuck into the wall next to him.

"Oh, balls!" he shouted before diving out of the way just in time to avoid being blown apart. He did not hear 17 laying down fire due to the ringing in his ears. With The Tank distracted Number 12 jumped up and ran toward the armored vigilante, placing a remote mine square on his back. The Tank turned and 17 herded the last surviving men out the door. Number 12 dove out a nearby window, hitting the detonator, blowing the building, and sending The Tank to whichever god it was he prayed to.

7/ THE BROTHERHOOD AGAINST TYRANNY

"Some people just have to persecute Truth."
–Damien Elkhart

Tyler Kelly had become increasingly distracted since the incident at Diamond Pharmaceuticals. He'd never killed anyone before, but just days before he'd blown a man apart. His actions had landed him a large bonus and a pay-rate bump. Offing vigilantes who made it their business to be perpetual thorns in the side of Damien Elkhart was always well rewarded. But Tyler's mind was not on his promotions or extra vacation time. It was on his first kill. After cooking dinner he found he'd left the oven on. It was hard not to focus on those unidentifiable remains encased in armor.

He had run out of underwear. This encouraged a somewhat past-due laundry day. Across the street from the laundromat was a bar. In need of a drink, Tyler reached for his wallet. An investigative patting revealed its absence. Panic set in as he realized his wallet was in yesterday's pants. He sprinted back to the Laundromat and threw open the washer door. He thrust his arms into the suds and water and pulled out the pants he'd had on yesterday. His wallet was there. It had contained his driver's license, library card, CPR certification, and $194 dollars cash, which had stuck together. He took it back down the street to his apartment and carefully separated the bills. He sat on the couch and dried out the saturated contents of his wallet with a blow-dryer while watching television.

The news was on. Stories about the explosion at the pharmaceutical lab were still all over the television. Diamond Pharmaceuticals' bankruptcy and theories of terrorist involvement were all anyone could talk about. They weren't far from the truth. One other major breaking story began to emerge.

"This just in," said the pretty, young, multi-Emmy award winning minority female journalist. "Heavyweight Champion Butch London has been missing for three days."

This caught Tyler's attention. He shut off the hair dryer and turned up the volume.

"Butch London, considered the greatest heavyweight fighter in the world, failed to show up for his fight with Cedric Ramirez last night," she continued. "The fighter was well known for his extremely private personal life. Butch London's only known living relative is inventor Howard London..."

"Shit. I had money on that fight," Tyler said out loud to no one in particular. He'd almost forgotten about it, his mind had been on the man he'd killed only days earlier.

"We go now to a live press conference being held by Howard London."

A tall, well-dressed African-American man stood behind a podium and adjusted his glasses as he cleared his throat. "My brother is a private man. But it is no secret that he had a lot of enemies. Foul-play in his disappearance is a possibility we are taking very seriously."

The newscaster continued: "The gambling commission has gone on record saying that 'Obviously all bets are off on the London versus Ramirez fight.' The fight will be postponed until further notice."

The disappearance of Butch London prompted a lot of water cooler chit chat at Elkhart Global Dynamics. So had Number 12's defeat of The Tank. He couldn't walk down the hall without someone patting him on the shoulder.

"Good one, bro," Number 52 said.

"Hey! Look at the balls on that guy!" said 45.

Number 9 merely touched him on the shoulder as she walked past. He turned to look at her and she gave a subtle smile.

Number 17 approached 12 and shook his hand. "Hey, man. You holding up alright?"

"Yeah, sure. Why wouldn't I be?"

"Dunno. Massive explosion? Co-workers dying? Killing a man? Ringing any bells?"

"Well, apparently those are things we'll have to get used to," 12 reminded him. They began to make their way to the locker rooms. 12 opened his locker. The inside of the door held a favorite comic strip and a magnetic mirror with a small corner broken off. "So, how are you planning to spend your bonus money?"

"My sister's college. Tuition for second semester is due next week." Number 17 slipped into his bulletproof vest.

"How much is that up to?" 12 loaded his gun.

"Too damn," Number 17 double-checked his gun sight. "That's how much."

"I hear you on that one." 12 shut his locker. The pair made their way to the briefing room.

"How much do you owe?"

"Too damn," 12 echoed. They both laughed.

As they entered the briefing room, everyone stood up and applauded them. Number 12 gave a few little bows. Number 17 followed his example and added blowing kisses.

"Thank you, thank you!" 12 said, "No, no. We were just doing our jobs."

"Okay, okay," said Number 62 as he put out a cigarette on the podium. "If we're done tugging on the heroes' dicks, I'd like to get started."

He began by lighting another one. "Okay," he said prior to being interrupted by a knocking at the door. A representative from Human Resources entered. The man possessed a deformity reminiscent of a Dick Tracy villain; he had no discernible face. The men went silent. Some looked at their shoelaces to avoid staring. Others simply succumbed to gawking.

"Sorry to interrupt," he said, "But I need to speak to a Number," he paused a moment as he checked his clipboard and flipped through the pages rhythmically, "12."

"We are about to have a briefing here," Number 62 protested.

"Postpone it," The Faceless Man said. "This should only take a few minutes."

"Bullshit!" 62 spit on the floor.

The Faceless Man from H.R. showed him a packet of paper. 62 scowled as he flipped through it. He mumbled something about "goddamn pussies."

"Okay, everybody," Number 62 said. "Take five. Grab a coffee or a cigarette, take a piss, and be back here by a quarter after."

Number 12 followed the man downstairs to the Human Resources offices in the basement. No words were exchanged during the elevator ride. Number 12 resisted the urge to ask how or why the man had no face. Damned if it wasn't creepy, though. Like a spy movie villain.

When they reached the offices, the man sat behind his bland, albeit neatly kept desk. There were no photos or decorations on the walls. He motioned for Number 12 to sit down. So Number 12 did. Whatever device existed in the base of the swivel chair that kept it from leaning back was broken. Number 12 had to shift his weight in a rather uncomfortable fashion to keep from falling back.

"We're just doing a follow up here," The Faceless Man explained.

"Okay," said 12. There was a lingering silence.

"Well? I understand you had a few firsts recently. It's company policy to follow up on these things. So, how are you?"

"Umm... okay I guess," Number 12 replied.

"You guess?"

"Yeah. I mean, it comes with the territory, right?"

"Yes," the man assured him, "It certainly does." This was followed by Number 12 simply biting his lower lip and nodding.

"Well, that's about it then. Come down if you need anything and we can refer you to a counselor."

"Okay," Number 12 said. He closed the door behind him.

On his way back to the briefing room, Number 12 stopped for a cup of water at the cooler by the break room. On the wall was a framed poster of a spider in the middle of a massive web. It read "Commitment: Starting Something and Sticking to It." 12 could only assume some sort of pun was involved.

"Hey, 12," said Number 101, "You hear about Butch London?"

"Yeah," Number 12 said. "Saw it on the news last night. Fucked up, no?"

"Fucked up is right," 101 concurred. "I had money on that fight too."

"You and me both," Number 12 took a sip of water.

"I also hear you off'd The Tank."

"You heard right."

"How'd you pull that one off?"

"Oh, timing, teamwork... a little bit of luck. You know how it is."

"No. No I don't. Never killed a full-fledged hero before."

"Yeah, well... you're missing out." Number 12 crumpled up his cup and tossed it toward the waste basket. It spun around the edge of the rim before jumping back out and falling to the floor.

"Hey!" 101 shouted after. "Throw your trash in the basket, man!"

"Not now. Got a meeting," Number 12 said over his shoulder and he rounded the corner.

As he approached the briefing room, Number 62 approached him. "Get your touchy feely pussy shit out of the way?"

"Blow it out your ass, Cock Wrinkle," Number 12 said as he passed, tossing the door open.

Number 62 caught the door handle, "Good answer."

Number 12 took his seat next to 17.

"What was that about?" 17 wanted to know.

"They were just 'checking up on me.' Y'know, that kinda' thing," 12 explained.

"Enough gossip. We're behind schedule as it is. On today's menu: assault and invasion," he said as the lights went off and the projector went on. "The B.A.T., or Brotherhood Against Tyranny, has been a thorn in our side for a number of years now. They are a militant group battling world domination and corporate monopolies. We don't like them."

"Why not?" Someone in the back asked.

"They have successfully thwarted several of our projects in the past. And so we are hitting them back. Now if the stupid questions are out of the way. It will be a full-on assault on their compound. The first wave will come in from above. That will be covered by our associates who have the appropriate airborne training. They are getting their briefing down the hall. You will be the second wave. We will swarm through the windows as The B.A.T is distracted by the first wave."

Number 17 raised his hand, "Excuse me."

"What?" 62 said with an irritated tone.

"With this plan won't the casualty rate be extremely high?"

"The Board of Directors has approved the outline," 62 explained without answering the question. "Moving on. The objective is to do as much damage to their base of operations as humanly possible. Ideally we want even more than that. We want our enemies to truly feel they have suffered the wrath of God. So that's what we will bring. If we do this right, we may even take them down permanently."

They had not taken down The B.A.T. permanently. What did happen could only be accurately described as "disastrous." The company would describe it as "having dropped the ball"; a testament to their ability to churn out euphemisms, a talent that should truly never be underestimated.

The metaphorical ass-fucking was inevitable from the very beginning. It boiled down to the simple fact that the intelligence received was abysmal. The information given to them was poorly researched, poorly scouted, and poorly interpreted.

By the time 12 and 17 had burst in through the window, most of the first wave had already been taken down. It wasn't that The B.A.T. knew they were coming. Or that they were even ready for them. Intelligence had sorely underestimated the numbers and the abilities of the Brotherhood. But, perhaps most importantly, there was very little about the layout of the facility that Intelligence had gotten right. This had put the Elkhart assault team at a severe disadvantage. Hallways they believed led to key attack areas instead led to dead ends that became more than a figure of speech.

"Holy living fuck!" proclaimed 12 as they were rushed by a B.A.T. tactical guard unit that wasn't supposed to be there. Taking quick cover in a doorway, he rolled a grenade down the hall. There was a loud bang and several limbs donning B.A.T.'s trademark dark leather flew by.

"Where the hell did they come from?" 17 said from somewhere. 12 looked and saw 17 had taken cover behind an open door across the hall.

"How the fuck would I know?" 12 yelled back. "Something's fucked," he then added, stating what they both already knew. A bullet whizzed by, hitting the ground inches from Number 12's hand. He responded by blindly firing a few rounds down the hall.

"Somebody really dropped the mother-fucking ball on this one," 17 theorized.

"Y'think?"

"Nothing about this adds up at all. It's not us, right? I mean, I paid attention. But this..."

"...is all wrong. Yeah," 12 finished before three more shots hit the wall a mere inch or two from his head. "Sons of bitches!" He yelled, poking his head out in an ill-advised fashion, and spray fired down the hall. 17 tackled him as bullets whizzed back, catching one in the leg in the process.

"Shit!" He shouted.

"Are you hit?" 12 asked.

"Ugh. Yeah. Just my leg though." 17 said.

12 ripped off his sleeve and fashioned a makeshift tourniquet, stopping the bleeding. A garbled message came in over the communicator built into their helmets.

"12, 17, where the fuck are you?"

"We're pinned down" 12 said, "17's hit. Just the leg. I've stopped the bleeding."

"We're fucking dying over here," the communicator said.

"Where are you?" 17 asked. The response was unintelligible.

"How many grenades you have?" 12 asked 17.

"I got three."

"Okay. I'm down to two. Throw one and I'll lay down some fire to cut down their chances of jumping out of the way of the blast. Right after you throw, you lay down fire and I'll throw. Then we do it again. Lather, rinse, repeat. Got that?"

"What if our guys are down there too?" 17 wanted to know.

"If there are, they're already dead," said 12.

Though a dent was put in The B.A.T.'s numbers, the mission was still regarded as a failure. Number 62 came storming into the offices with eyes and cigarette burning.

"What in the name of the Holy Piss of Christ was that?" He screamed.

"Sir," the male administrative assistant said, "this is a non-smoking office. Please put out your cigarette and..." Number 62 pushed him into the wall as he put his cigarette out on the man's forehead. The man let out a scream of pain.

Some higher-ups ran out to check on the situation. "What is going on here?"

"My unit got torn apart all because the intelligence you gave us was bullshit!" Number 62 yelled. "The hell were you trying to pull?"

"Number 62, I assure you we are not trying to pull anything. If you come with me and fill out the necessary paperwork, we'll take care of it."

They guided Number 62 down the hall to a small room. There was a folding chair and an old desk. They handed him a ballpoint pen and a stack of papers.

"We need you to fill out these forms. Fill out pages 2, 5, 6, 7, 9, 13,14, 15, 18, 21, and 25-45. But only the top sections of 27, 28, 29, and 35. And only the bottom parts of 37, 38, 39, and 42. The rest is for office use only and pages 46-50 are to be filled out by both the office and employee together after both parties have filled out their respective parts. Let us know when you have your part completed."

They shut the door on Number 62. The air-conditioner hummed. The pen was out of ink.

8/ GIRL TALK

"We all know what drives people. Why not take the wheel?"
–Damien Elkhart

When Number 9 met her, Kathy was already known as Number 3. Kathy was about five years older, an age difference that seemed less significant with time. They trained together, they did assignments together. They were considered, in the circles that consider such things, to be the two deadliest women under twenty-five.

It was clear to Number 3, and all who saw them together, that Number 9 looked to her as a surrogate sister; a female role model in a lifetime of male abusers, albeit a considerably unconventional one.

"Any good ones in the new batch?" Number 3 asked 9 while walking the hall a few days after orientation.

"I dunno. One of them was kinda cute, in that scruffy sort of way..."

"Mmm," Number 3 held open the locker room doors, "Light beard, perpetual bed head... you do have a type, don't you? What his number?"

"Does it matter? You know the policy. Besides, I'm just glad I'm done with recruiting," 9 said.

"For now at least. How long does this batch look like it will last?" Number 3 removed a leather catsuit from her locker.

"Hard to say," said 9, slipping into her suit. "It always is. Let's just get this done, okay?"

"Whatever you say."

Less than a half hour later they were crawling through the vents of an office building on a standard espionage mission with the goal of information retrieval. The girls were infiltrating a rival company. This company specialized in the development of monitoring equipment used in surveillance satellites. It had slipped out that the company was on the verge of a major breakthrough with tracking devices. The girls were to confirm or deny the rumors and, if the hearsay proved true, steal any records including plans and test data.

Their infiltration gear was standard. This included tight-fitting leather jumpsuits with a low V cut.

"I understand why it has to be so tight-fitting," 9 commented. "But what's with cleavage?"

Number 3 carefully brought the air vent up so it would not fall to the floor. "Got it," she said. "Yeah," she concurred. "It doesn't seem very practical, does it?"

"Sexist pigs must have designed them." With quiet grace they slipped to the floor. Their landings didn't make a sound.

"I mean... ," 9 whispered as she held her tits to emphasize the cleavage, "only a man, right?"

Number 3 tried to keep her giggle volume down. "For sure."

"I'm sure they just love watching us leave for a mission..." As 9 said this she sauntered around the office with her butt out.

"Shhh!" said 3. "Stop it. You'll make me laugh."

"Relax. We disabled all the alarms."

"Yeah, but there's still security guards."

"This place just looks like a standard office building," Number 9 commented.

"This place is just a standard office building. But they do a lot of data entry here." 3 typed away at a computer, being the superior hacker of the two. "Just keep an eye out."

There were several minutes of silence. Number 9 jiggled her boobs. "Ridiculous," she muttered to herself.

"Got it," said 3.

"Hold it," said a security guard.

"Shit," said one girl.

"Fuck," said the other.

"What are you two doing?" The security guard said, pointing his assault rifle. The guard was too heavily armed for it to be a standard office building. He knew what he was guarding. "Who are..." he hesitated. It quickly became apparent he was staring directly at Number 9's chest. Taking this opportunity Number 3 drew her silenced pistol and shot the guard in the head. Within seconds they were both back in the vent with the payload on disk. They suppressed their laughter until they were in the car and the hell out of Dodge. After a few moments Number 9 let loose and was bawling with laughter. Number 3 joined her friend and had to pull over for fear of crashing the car.

"What are you doing?" 9 said through tears of laughter. "Drive. Get us the fuck out of here."

"Sorry, sorry." Number 3 chuckled. She took some deep breaths and started driving again.

"Seems a little more practical now, doesn't it?" 3 said after awhile.

"Yeah," said 9. "Still... men. Right? I mean, same situation, reversed. If they put a huge bulge in the crotch of the guys' sneaking suits to throw off female guards..."

Number 3 started to laugh again.

"Can you imagine? It would never work. That shit only works on men."

"I know, right?" 3 concurred.

A few moments passed.

"I'd probably look," 3 said.

"Yeah. Me too."

9/THE IL'BAL

"Ancient societies saw what we cannot."
–Damien Elkhart

12 and 17 found themselves working together again. They were in the Amazon searching for what archeologists called "Site Q," a site that was believed to be a treasure trove of Mayan artifacts. Specifically they were seeking the Il'bal, the Mayan "instrument for seeing." Damien Elkhart believed this device was crucial in showing the world what only he knew. His pursuit of the Truth was relentless and it had taken him, and consequently the henchmen, to all corners of the Earth.

"At least I'm seeing the world," 12 muttered to himself.

"I fucking hate the jungle," Number 17 said. They had just spent the last several hours standing in the sweltering heat being lectured on the importance of changing their socks frequently and why wearing underpants was ill advised (it had long been established that the words "crotch rot" grab even the most fickle attention spans).

"Yeah," said 12, "But the unfurnished basement is fantastic. I may never go back."

"I hear there's a fish in the river that lodges itself in your dick and lays its eggs there," Number 17 commented. Everyone in earshot crossed their legs uncomfortably. "Don't piss off the side of the boats. They can swim up your piss stream."

"That's not true," 12 contradicted.

Numbers 83 and 45 glanced over their shoulders, rolling their eyes at the conversation.

"Believe what you want, but I'm pissing into a can and throwing it over the side."

"That's horrible!" exclaimed Number 23. "This isn't even my job. I shouldn't be here!"

"Why are you here?" asked 12, "Aren't you, like, the computer guy or something?"

"Correct," 23 held his gun wrong. "But someone called in sick at the last minute. So they asked me to fill in. If I had known I'd be sent to the middle of South America, I would have declined. I was even hesitant. But they kept saying 'Be a team-player, 23!' and so I said 'Okay'."

"Chill out," 17 told him.

"God doesn't want me to be here. Why didn't I listen to him?" 23 groaned.

"I don't know much about that stuff," 12 said, "But shouldn't you believe that you being here is part of God's plan or something?"

"I'd hate to interrupt this little book club meeting," 62 breathed out cigar smoke all over 23, who coughed, "but we're rolling out of here soon. You all paid attention to the lecture?"

"I'm going commando as we speak," said 12 as he twisted his hips as if using a hula-hoop. "Woo-hoooo!"

62 rolled his eyes then spit. "Good. You don't want your balls to rot off." He walked away.

"I already feel like my balls have rotted off," 17 commented. "I don't know how much longer I can do this shit."

"Just remember why you took the job," offered 23.

"Yeah," 12 said, "think about Sarah. I always do." He made a masturbation pantomime.

"Hey! Watch it! That's my sister you're talking about!"

"Sorry. But your sister is really cute," 12 said.

Several days before, Number 12 had met Number 17's sister. It was a chance meeting. The two had wandered into the same bar after work one Friday night. There was a place near Elkhart Global headquarters called The Capitol where a number of minions would go to knock a few back after work. The decor of the establishment consisted of paintings of the Second Continental Congress. There were also framed prints of various documents such as the Constitution and Declaration of Independence. Miniatures of monuments sat next to the bottles on the shelf behind the bar.

"Hey!" said 17.

"What's going on?" 12 responded.

"How's it hanging, hero slayer?" 17 asked.

"Flaccid, sweaty. Slightly to the left."

"Graphic. Join me for a pitcher?" 17 offered.

"Why not? But seriously, that shit with The Tank was dumb luck..."

"Don't be modest." 17 signaled the bartender. "Play it up and you'll go somewhere."

"I guess. But you helped," 12 pointed out. The bartender placed the pitcher and two frosty glasses in front of them. "Look," said 12, "don't take this the wrong way. But you're not a fag are you?"

"What? No. You can buy the next round if you want," 17 responded. "I'm not trying to pick you up or anything."

12 just laughed. "I know. I'm giving you shit."

"Oh. Well... good?" They both laughed and poured their beers.

"Cheers," said 12 and they clicked glasses. 12 took a sip. 17 answered his ringing cell phone.

"Hey," 17 said. "Yeah. I'm at The Capitol." He laughed, "No, no. The bar across from work." Number 17 took a sip. "What? You are?" 17 listened for a moment. "Sure, swing on by. See you." 17 hung up.

"Girlfriend?" 12 asked.

"Sister," said 17. Some time passed and through the door walked a thin, full-lipped young woman. Her hair was short and dyed with purple highlights.

"Hey, Bro," she said, giving him a hug. She noticed Number 12.

"Oh," said 17, "Sarah this is Number 12. We work together."

"Oh right," Sarah laughed. "You guys have to do that number thing. Ka-, I mean 17 told me all about it."

"My friends call me T.K.," said 12, offering his hand to her.

"Nice to meet you, 12," she said smiling.

17 noticed the flirtatious look on his sister's face. He dug into his pocket and pulled out a piece of paper and handed it to her.

"Here's that info you needed, Sis," he said.

"Thanks!" She said, giving it a look over, "See you at home, Bro. See you around, Number 12."

Number 12 watched as Sarah Jenson walked out of the door.

"Are you looking at my sister's ass?" 17 asked.

"I am," said 12. He sipped his beer.

The jungle had the kind of heat that made one feel sticky. Fortunately the uniforms provided to the henchmen were conducive to the climate. Still, only so many advancements had been made in the science of fabric development, and the men began to feel the effects of the sweltering jungle heat.

"My balls are stuck to the side of my leg," Number 12 said.

"Thank you," said 17. "Thank you for that."

"Seriously," said 12. "It even kinda' stings."

"That is so inappropriate," said 23.

"Know how the saltiness of your sweat starts to hurt when..."

"Yes," said 17, "I'm fully aware of it. I, too, have ball sweat. I just don't feel the need to share my struggle with the world."

"I just want to see how much the computer guy can listen to," 12 explained. However, Number 23 had long since covered his ears and had even started to sing.

"Our Gooood is an awesome God. He reeeeeigns in Heaven above..."

Number 62 stood at the front of the boat. He would stare down at the map in his hands and then scan the riverbed. A particular rock formation caught his eye, and he signaled the driver to pull the boat over to the side. The boat hit the riverbed with a force that threw many of the men off balance.

"This looks like the place, gentlemen," shouted 62, using the term loosely. "I want a good, thorough sweep of the area surrounding these formations. We're looking for anything that might be an entrance."

The orders were vague, which was common.

"What looks like it might be an entrance?" 12 wondered out loud.

"Got me," 17 said. "Maybe we'll know when we see it?"

"One can only hope," said 12. He ran his hand along the rock formations. Something about it seemed odd. "This isn't a natural formation," he said.

"What do you mean?" asked 17.

He brushed away dirt with his hands and scratched at the cracks in the formation.

"I think we got something here!" Number 12 shouted. Number 62 pushed his way through the men.

"What? What is it?"

"These formations might be the entrance to the temple. If you scratch around these cracks..."

"We'll take it from here," 62 interrupted. He pulled out a walkie-talkie which gave out an annoying chirp. "Historians to the formation. Get your well educated asses over here now."

The Historians were the research squad. They consisted of a number of eggheads specializing in archeology and anthropology. They were always crucial in these kinds of projects. They came running over with their computers and texts and began to point and squabble.

"Okay, everybody," 62 shouted, "give the brains some room to work."

The men wandered back to the boats. Number 12 kicked a rock into the river. It hit with a plop that stirred a number of the piranha. Another man, Number 83, was looking over 12's shoulder.

"Damn, man," was all he said.

"Hey!' 62 yelled, "Secure the perimeter."

"Secure it from what? The monkeys?"

"Don't give me shit, Number 12. We're not the only ones looking for this stuff."

The henchmen patrolled the area, not sure what they were patrolling for. Number 83 had been keeping an eye on the riverbank and saw something that looked suspicious. Another boat was tied to a tree a few yards away. Before Number 83 could investigate further, he saw Drake Rodgers. Drake Rodgers was a famous treasure hunter and archeologist. Rodgers was in the employ of the United States government to track down and obtain mystical objects that the U.S. did not want to fall into the wrong hands. What Elkhart was digging for fit that bill.

Number 83 lifted his gun, but Rodgers was faster. Rodgers threw his knife and it stuck into 83's gun, ruining it. Rodgers closed the space quickly, striking 83 on the jaw. He recovered and kicked Rodgers in the chest. He landed a few more blows to Drake Rodgers's face. The riverbank was raised and there was a ten foot drop down into the water. However, the men were too engaged in their melee combat to take this into consideration. Drake Rodgers charged at 83, leaping into the air, grabbed a branch, and, in an unnecessarily acrobatic display, swung toward 83 and kicked him. Number 83 stumbled backwards, falling off the cliff and into the river. As 83 tried to swim back to the water's edge, he felt a sharp pain in his leg.

"Fuck!" 83 felt the sharp pain again and then again in quick succession, "Jesus! Fuck!" He'd come across a school of piranha. In less than a minute, he was just bone.

The Historians had figured out how to open the temple doors, and so the men were called back. A few remained on patrol and were told to keep an eye out for Number 83. Both 12 and 17 were on the team that was to search the temple. A horrendous musk permeated the air. Number 23's asthma kept him from noticing the wonders held within the subterranean temple.

"Shouldn't we be wearing masks or something?" Number 12 asked. "I mean there's got to be some sort of mold-borne pathogens or something. This place hasn't been aired out in hundreds of years."

About half a dozen men wandered in and followed the twisting tunnels. One of the Historians spoke up.

"Easy," he said. "Some of these booby-traps may still be active after all these years."

The men admired the treasures and the Historians looked in awe at the paintings on the wall, which seemed to unravel the story of the artifacts in question. To the untrained eye, they seemed very vague. They depicted many identical people on their knees. In front of them stood a man with an elaborate headdress holding an orb above his head.

"Oh, shit," said Number 20, "I just stepped on something."

"Nobody move!" said 62. "Nobody fucking move!" After that there was a creaking sound. "Everybody run!" 62 shouted. As they ran spikes came in from the wall. A hole opened in the ground and 12 and 17 fell in and slid down a steep slope that took them to the inner sanctum.

"Ow," Number 12 moaned.

"My ass," said 17.

"You landed on your ass?" 12 asked. "You lucky bastard. My head is... am I bleeding?"

17 clicked on his flashlight and looked at 12's head. "No," he told him, "Just a nasty bump. But that doesn't change the fact we're trapped."

"There must be some kinda way out of here," 12 said. They shined their lights, showing no way out except for the hole they fell from. "Shit," said 12. "Shit, shit, and shit again."

"We wait," said 17, having regained some composure. "If they want that artifact they'll have to come through here again,"

"Wish I had some wood to knock on," said 12.

Time passed and 12 and 17 sat with their backs against the wall.

"So," said Number 12, "Tell me a bit about yourself."

"What do you mean?"

"I mean, there's a chance we'll die down here. So I figure, fuck it. What's your deal?"

"I dunno..."

"My name is Tyler Kelly," Number 12 said.

"Shut up. Don't tell me your name... ," 17 said.

"No, fuck this Number 12 shit. I'm Tyler fucking Kelly and now you know that. So deal with it."

There was an awkward pause for a few minutes before Number 17 held out his hand.

"Karl Jenson," he said.

"So, that makes your sister Sarah Jenson."

"Brilliant, Holmes."

Tyler laughed. "So, you two seem really close. You're helping support her, right?"

"Yeah, well. Our parents are dead, and we're kinda all the other's got. She's in college, second year. I'm helping her pay for it."

"That's awful nice of you," said Tyler.

"Well, I didn't get to go. I was too busy working trying to put food on our table. I really want her to go further, y'know?"

"So you've been taking care of her and yourself?"

"Yeah,"

"Damn, man."

"What?"

"Nothing. Just, damn."

"Well, family is family. It's why I took the job," Karl said.

"Sounds noble enough," Tyler nodded.

"How about you? Why'd you take this shit job?"

"Nothing near as dramatic," said Tyler, "I'm trying to put a dent in my student loans. That's what I get for going to college for my art, right?"

"What did you go to school for?" Karl asked.

"Writing," said Tyler.

"What kind of stuff do you write?"

"Why does everybody ask that?" said Tyler with a little more attitude than was necessary.

"Just seems like the natural progression of the conversation is all."

"I'm thirsty," said Tyler. "Can people drink their own urine?"

"Sure," said Karl, "As long as it's your own."

Tyler and Karl were not sure exactly how much time had gone by, but after a day or two they heard voices from above. There were sounds of loud drilling; they looked up and saw lights.

"Down here!" they shouted.

They squinted as a spotlight shined down on them.

"12 and 17," 62 called down, "Is that you?"

"Yeah!" 12 called up. "Get us out of here!"

"We're sending down a harness," 62 said.

A vest on the end of a cable was lowered into the pit.

"Well, 17?" said 12. "You first."

As soon as they were both out, they were taken to the medical tent and treated for their wounds and given food and water. They were handed injury report forms and asked to fill them out.

"We just need a record that says your wounds were dressed in the field. We'll be taking you back to the States for further care."

"I think we'll be alright," said 12.

"I'm afraid I have to insist. Liability purposes and whatnot."

12 and 17 were carted back to the boats to be taken home, and the rest of the men descended into the temple.

"Looks like we're missing out," said 17.

"To Hell with that. I've had enough of the goddamn Mayans for a while," said 12, taking a sip of water from a bottle.

10/ BREAK ROOM COFFEE

"I've seen the things you missed."
–Damien Elkhart

Break room coffee tastes like shit. Numbers 12 and 17 sat in the staff lounge several days after returning from South America. The doctors had checked them out, taking blood and performing tests which involved actions that would have required dinner and a movie under other circumstances. Aside from some mild damage to the lungs from the mold in the tomb (for which they were given medication), they were fine and cleared as okay to return to work. Number 23 entered and filled up a bottle at the water cooler.

"23!" they both harmonized.

Startled, he turned around. "Thank the Lord!" He proclaimed, "Thank the good Lord you two are okay!"

"Yeah," said 12. "Props to the G-man."

"Woo!" said 17 flatly, giving a raise-the-roof gesture.

"What happened to you two?" 23 asked.

"Nothing special," said 17. "They brought us back to the States, had the doctors make sure we didn't pick up some kind of unknown ancient tropical sicknesses or curses. Gave us some inhalers to use for a couple weeks and sent us back to work."

"I'm more interested to hear what happened after we left," said 12.

"Yeah," 17 chimed in, "Did they find the Iqbal?"

"The Il'bal," 12 corrected him. "Iqbal was a Muslim philosopher poet."

"Ooh... college boy," mocked 17. "Does it give you pleasure correcting dumb people?"

"Buddy, it's practically orgasmic," said 12, sipping his coffee victoriously.

"Did you find the Il'bal?" 17 said again, turning to 12 as he said "Il'bal" with added venom.

"Oh we found it all right," said 23 as he took a seat. "But I'm just glad to be back behind the computers where I belong."

"Ever find out God's reason for sending you there?" asked 17.

"Not really," said 23. "I mean, they could've just as easily done it without me."

"So what happened? What'd we miss?"

"Well, the deeper parts of the temple were stunning. Especially the ceremonial altars. I didn't know enough about what I was looking at to understand the drawings on the walls, but it looked like some kind of details of the ritual. We found some sort of crack, or actually more like a crease, in the wall. And it looked like some kind of a doorway. The demo-squad came down and used some plastic explosives and lined the crease with it and blew a hole in the wall. There was this path leading down. And I heard someone saying that was where the Il'bal was stored."

"Were there any booby-traps?" asked 12.

"It looked like there were, but I mean the temple is thousands of years old. And it's been who-knows-how-long since anyone set foot in there. Most of them didn't work anymore. Everything being so old was dangerous enough.

"The historians kept looking at texts under flashlights and pointing at drawings on the wall. They were saying how it was where the Il'bal was kept, and it was believed to still be there. So we get down to the bottom, and you'll never guess who was there!"

"Liam Adams?" asked 12.

"Members of The B.A.T.?" 17 guessed.

"Duke Rodgers!" 23 said.

"Freelance treasure hunter Drake Rodgers?" said 12, somewhat surprised.

"Sorry, yeah. Drake..."

"I heard the Neo-Nazis dispatched him in Cairo," said 17.

"That's what I'd heard," said 12, "but half the crap the Neo-Nazis say is bullshit. It's all propaganda with those guys."

"So, Rodgers is holding the thing, right?"

"The Iq-," 17 corrected himself, "Il'bal?"

"Yeah. And he sees us standing there. And everyone just aims at him, all the guns are clicking. I didn't know how to work mine so I just pointed it."

"They didn't teach you how?" 12 asked.

"No," said 23.

"What the fuck is that?" asked 12. "I mean how the Hell do they expect you to do a job when they don't even train you? It's asinine!"

"Hey, 12," interrupted 17.

"What!?!"

"The story," 17 reminded him.

"Oh, yeah. Sorry. Go on."

"So he sees us standing there and realizes he's got no way out. So he's about ready to smash the Il'bal..."

"What did it look like?" asked 12.

"The picture is around. You haven't seen it yet?"

"No."

"It's oval. It's a sort of crystal. But it's a strange color, kinda blueish with a purple middle. It looks like a big eyeball. Anyway... he's going to smash it. But then Damien Elkhart himself steps forward."

"I didn't even realize Elkhart was there," said 17.

"He didn't show till after you two were sent home."

"Oh."

"So he steps forward and he snaps his fingers, and Number 45 comes in and he's got this girl tied up and Elkhart grabs her and says something like 'Easy now, Drake. I don't want to hurt the girl. If you do anything stupid, she dies. And, boy... you're gonna carry that weight a long time.'"

"Who was the girl?" 17 wanted to know.

"I don't know. I'd never seen her before. But you know how Rodgers is. It's a different girl each time. You'd think he was a Mormon."

"Did you just make a joke?" 12 asked.

23 merely shrugged sheepishly.

"I'd say that's a big step forward," said 17. "Wouldn't you agree, Number 12?"

"They grow up so fast, don't they, Honey?" 12 cooed.

"So what happened next?" 17 said after he finished laughing.

"He went to toss it to Elkhart and Elkhart put up one finger and said, 'Careful now!' Elkhart threw the girl to one of the other men... Number 30, I think. Rodgers tossed the Il'bal to Elkhart and Elkhart caught it. He took both of them into custody and someone tied 'em up. They flew in a different plane than me. Then we came home."

"When'd you get back?" said 17.

"Last night."

"Well, we gotta get back. We got a briefing in five. But glad to see you made it back safe," said 17.

"'Yea, though I walk through the valley of the shadow of death, I fear no evil for thou art with me.' Psalm 23:4,'" 23 quoted. "God would never put me in harm's way. Not so long as I have faith."

Number 12 and Number 17 both nodded awkwardly.

"Well, see ya," 17 said and then headed down the hall with Number 12.

As Number 23 sat and ate his lunch, he hummed a song. It was off key but sounded like "Onward Christian Soldiers."

11/ LIAM ADAMS

"Until you find something to die for, you have nothing to live for."
—Damien Elkhart

Kathy had been with Elkhart Global Dynamics for a long time. Much like Lucy Morgan, the luscious Number 9, she'd been schooled in Elkhart's Truth. She'd dedicated her life to it. That was until she first encountered a charming, brash young agent named Liam Adams. Adams would set into motion that which would lead to Kathy Donaldson's treachery and forever assure that he would be a thorn in Damien Elkhart's side.

The reality must be left up to speculation. There were numerous theories about how she turned. The first revolves around her relationship with Damien Elkhart. It was a well known fact that Damien Elkhart had a special level of admiration for Kathy. Whereas Kathy had a certain kind of love for Damien, it was more like that of a sister for a big brother, a daughter for a father, or a parishioner for a preacher. His growing advances became difficult for her. He called her "My Magdalene." It made her uncomfortable and made it difficult for her to do her job. The incident that put her over the edge came with Damien's attempt to propose to her.

He had invited her to sit down over a lamb dinner, as he often did when he had important matters to discuss.

"Katherine," he said as he opened a small box, "You are going to be my wife."

"I don't think that's the best idea," she'd said. Damien Elkhart was not a man who took rejection well. Disagreement for Elkhart was devastation.

"I have seen us together in the future, Katherine. It is destiny!" He grew belligerent.

"Damien, I'm sorry. But you are like a brother to me and it would get in the way..."

"I know what is to be! You know nothing! This is part of the plan!"

"I should leave now, Damien. You're not thinking clearly." She put her utensils down and stood up.

"I do nothing but think clearly. You are the one who is willingly going against what is meant to be. You are defying destiny! If you defy what I know to be true..."

"What are you saying?"

Damien's eyes flared up with a level of intensity that she had never seen before, and it was terrifying. He pointed at her with one hand and opened a drawer with the other.

"You would never say such a thing... If you knew," he said. "You must be fixed," he said, "and I shall fix you." He picked up his knife and quickly moved toward her. "I know what I..."

Katherine did not let Damien Elkhart finish that sentence. She pushed her chair into him and ran out of the building. It is believed that this incident drove her to break away from the Elkhart Ideology and inspired her to destroy that which she helped build. But again, this was only speculation. Whispers around the office.

The first time that Kathy Donaldson met Liam Adams was some time before the alleged incident with Damien Elkhart. Adams was infiltrating one of Elkhart's "Education Facilities." It was at these locations that employees who had been with the company a number of years were educated in Damien Elkhart's vision of "The Truth." In hopes of obtaining clues to the company's plots, Liam Adams infiltrated in order to steal recorded materials pertaining to Elkhart's dogma. Adams was convinced if he could verse himself in his enemy's beliefs, he might be able to predict his enemy's actions. He was seeking notes, recordings, manifestos, or anything that outlined Elkhart's plans, beliefs, or teachings. An Elkhart Bible would be the Holy Grail. After cutting security wiring he jumped up into the air duct system. Much to his dismay part of the air ducts were secured by a laser system. Resourceful chap that he was, he had a small mirror as part of his tool set (the intended purpose was to signal planes if he needed rescuing). With a pocketknife and a bit of chewing gum, Liam Adams was able to slide the mirror into the lasers and reflect them back at their sources, frying them.

He carefully opened the vents, dropped down into the archives, and began to look around. Adams' arrogance had gotten the better of him yet again. He was not the full step ahead he had imagined himself to be. What he failed to factor into his equation was that Number 3 was sitting in the archives brushing up on Damien Elkhart's teachings. She spied him through the shelves. Though their paths had never crossed prior, his picture littered the walls of the break-rooms and offices, and his name was an echo at all briefings. He was wanted, but wanted alive.

Adams was hunched over, looking through the shelves. He flipped through notebooks, many of which he saw merely as the psychotic ravings of a madman, nothing tangible, nothing he could use.

"C'mon, c'mon... ," he muttered. "Where's it at?"

"Looking for this?" Number 3 said before bashing his head with her hardback, leather-bound Elkhart Bible. He fell to the ground, fazed but not unconscious.

"Christ almighty!" he proclaimed, rubbing the sore spot on the crown of his head.

She brought her leg down towards her victim with great force, which only worked against her as he caught her leg and swung her into the bookshelf, causing various volumes of text to fall to the tile floor.

Before she could retaliate, Adams had grabbed her by the throat and pinned her to the wall. His grasp was firm, but he was not choking her. Only when she struggled did he tighten his grip.

"Do you know who I am?" he asked.

She merely nodded in response.

"Then you should know I have no problem killing you," he reminded her.

"You should know I have no problem dying," she retorted.

Holding the Elkhart Bible up, he clenched his teeth "For this?"

She nodded.

"You're willing to die for this? For Elkhart? For what he wants?"

"If you haven't found something worth dying for," she quoted Elkhart's scripture, "You haven't found anything worth living for."

"You got it backwards, Luv," Liam Adams said, moving in closer. "Only when you've found something worth living for have you found something worth dying for." With this he kissed her hard and against her will. Before she could push him away, a smoke bomb went off. Number 3 heard the sound of shattering glass as she fell unconscious. Adams's words filled her brain as the smoke filled her lungs. She collapsed, coughing, and fell asleep.

Elkhart's words had held a truth for her. But so did Adams's. Two phrases in seeming direct contrast to each other vied for control of her being. Since both made sense, neither did. Everything spun, and she felt nauseous. Adams's dichotomy cut into her brain like the scalpel of a drunken surgeon. She pretended to shake it off. The ability to remain stoic in times of personal crisis was something imbued in her even before her training. It was part of why she fit the profile. After her fight with Damien Elkhart, it began to occur to her that the man she had so long admired was more than a little off his rocker. She knew he was a believer and she had no doubt that he was capable of doing something rash as a result of her turning him down. For her, switching sides was as much a means of survival as it was anything else. Having followed a diseased mind for so long raised a few questions about her own. "But first things first," Kathy thought. If her shattered confidence even deserved rebuilding, she could do that later. She sat down next to Number 9.

"You look out of it, Kat," said Lucy.

"Please, don't use my name while we're on the clock."

"Sorry, Number 3," she said, rolling her eyes, "But you seem like... not you."

"I can't talk about it here," Number 3 said, burying her face in her arms on the table.

"Well, let's go talk to Damien. He'll know just what to do," Number 9 suggested.

"I can't do that!" Number 3 screamed into her arms, muffling the sound. She looked up and Lucy saw her eyes tearing up. She had never seen tears in her friend's eyes.

"What? Why not? What happened? Kat, tell me what's going on!"

"I wish to Hell I could, Lucy," she said, having already composed herself. "Oh how I wish I could, honey." She hugged Lucy. "I love you, sweetie. Be careful."

She walked out before she lost her composure again. Lucy Morgan had not a clue to the situation. But she understood enough to realize her friend had just said, "Goodbye."

It took some work to track Liam Adams down, and it was hard for Kathy to avoid Damien, but she had done it. She found Adams on a riverboat casino and sat down across from him at the blackjack table where there were two other people. He looked up at her with subtle recognition as the dealer flipped out the cards with machine-like efficiency. He had thirteen; she had fifteen.

"Does your husband know you're here?" asked Adams, tapping the cards he had on the table. The dealer perfectly tossed another card. An eight. Blackjack.

"I'm not married anymore," she said. She tapped. A four brought her to nineteen. Everyone else busted.

"Now I can finally afford that sex change operation!" Adams proclaimed as the chips were slid to him. The rest of the table got up uncomfortably and left. Kathy took the seat next to him.

"And here I thought you were all about the ladies," she said.

"I just wanted the others to leave. Never underestimate how conservative Americans are when it comes to sexuality. The very thought of such things makes them all... whoo...," he mimicked a shudder.

"You're really fucked up, you know that?"

"That's almost a compliment coming from a follower of Elkhart," he quipped.

"That's actually what I came to talk to you about."

"It's not often you drug a woman and she calls you back," he said, pausing before sipping a drink. "Except maybe in university... sorry, college."

"Har-de-fucking-har. Are we going to have a serious discussion or what?"

"Anything for a lady," Adams said then turned to the dealer. "Hey, Chummly, take five." He tossed the dealer a hundred dollar chip.

"Chummly," whose name-tag read "Joe," nodded in gratitude and was about to leave before Liam Adams stopped him.

"Hang on," he sipped the last of his drink. "One more of these gin and tonics, you know how I like 'em. And for the lady?" He looked at

Kathy.

"No thanks," she said, "Nothing for me."

Adams gave her a look. "You on the clock or something?"

She paused only momentarily. "I'll have a Cosmo with Grey Goose, light on the pineapple juice and a twist."

"Attagirl," he said. "Now, what's this oh so serious discussion we need to have? More importantly why should-"

"I want out," she said.

"Door's over there. You're free to go," he said.

"No. I mean out of Elkhart Global Dynamics. I can't do it anymore."

"Outside," he said. "Now!"

He grabbed her arm and pulled her toward the door. Just then Chummly brought the drinks over. Kathy took hers and Adams left his. He blew right past Chummly.

"You forgot your drink," Kathy said. As they stormed through the casino, Liam Adams pulled out a poker chip and pressed the center of it. It sent a high voltage remote shock to the chip he'd given Chummly. Chummly fell to the ground and began convulsing. The contents of the spilled drink burned the carpet.

Another server approached Liam Adams with a drink, "Your gin and tonic, Mr. Adams, just how you like it." Adams tossed him the poker chip. He took the drink and downed it before heading into the alley.

"I don't know anything about that!" Kathy said.

"You wouldn't. It wasn't your people," he said.

"Ok, so why did you drag me out here?" she asked.

"To practice our rousing musical number," he quipped sarcastically. "To talk. No interruptions, no funny shit. What do you want from me?"

"I told you..."

"You told me jack-shit is what you told me. You just said 'I want out of Elkhart.' What does that have to do with me?" he said.

"I want to help you," she said.

"Just a few days ago you were trying to kill me and saying how you were ready to die for your beloved Damien and his cause! So you'll have to pardon me for being suspicious, Luv."

"Yeah, well. Something happened between then and now."

"A little lovers' spat, was there?"

She slapped him. Then grabbed his throat and pressed him against the wall.

"You cannot imagine the sleep I've lost."

"Oh but I can, Luv..."

"Shut up! I want out because I no longer believe in Damien. The man is completely insane!"

"Uh... yeah..."

She squeezed tighter. "His obsessions were starting to affect me in a very personal way. To a point that I feared for my safety and called into question everything I'd come to believe about myself and the world around me. He needs to be stopped."

"Given."

She leaned in real close. "I know things. Things you want to know..."

"You gonna kiss me too?"

She dropped him. "Boat's gonna sail."

He rubbed his neck. "Not bad..."

"Well?" she said.

"You got yourself a partner, Luv."

"For now we'll call it an 'uneasy alliance.'" She said, "One more thing... don't call me 'Luv.'"

"Anything for you, Doll," he said.

12/ THE ELKHART IDEAL

"Things have been decided."
–Damien Elkhart

The systems analyst formerly known as Dylan Roffredo sat at the console scrolling through lines of code. Having proven himself at this seemingly modest task a number of times, he'd been entrusted with double-checking the new targeting system.

"How's it coming, 23?"

He looked up from the screen. "Just fine, 122."

"Good, glad to hear it."

122 worked with Quality Assurance. Another so-called "egghead." It fell onto him to make sure the products being used by the company and shipped out to clients were up to "The Elkhart Ideal."

"Let's see what you've got." Number 122 looked over 23's shoulder and scrolled back through code. "What's this here?" 122 tapped the screen.

"Oh," 23 said, excited, "you'll like this. By making a few subtle tweaks, I've been able to increase accuracy by over ten percent!"

"Oh dear me," 122 muttered. He shook his head as he read through the altered code. "No. No, I'm afraid this will not do."

"Don't worry I ran tests on the simulations and everything. It works much better."

"No, no," said 122, "Change it back. The other way."

"But," 23 said, "this is better, much better. Not only does a more accurate targeting system turn a higher profit, but it ensures higher reliability and could save thousands of innocent lives by significantly reducing the chances of a misfire."

"Number 23," 122 explained, "here at Elkhart Dynamics we live by 'The Elkhart Ideal,' understand? It is devised and approved by top executives and Mr. Elkhart himself. This... other way... is not part of the 'Elkhart Ideal.'"

"But this showed to be an improvement time and time aga-"

"It is not up to the 'Elkhart Ideal' and must be changed back. Do you understand?"

23 did not understand.

"Yes," said 23, "I understand."

23 changed his flawed code back to the 'Elkhart Ideal.'

13/ ARMORY-43

"It is said, 'Shit happens.' But it has to. God doesn't make meaningless 'shit'."
–Damien Elkhart

One evening 12 and 17 were both guarding the east interior wall of Armory-43. 12 and 17 were standing about five yards apart. This made vocal conversation difficult considering they were under orders to remain silent. Every few minutes they would rotate. This was to keep any guards from spacing out. Number 109 had apparently fallen asleep on the job some months back and was terminated on the spot. Since then, the rotation policy had been amended to every ten minutes, as opposed to several hours of standing in the same place. As they passed, they would briefly exchange a joke.

"What do you call a cat that doesn't like to spend money?" 12 said quickly as they passed.

17 just shrugged as if to say, "I dunno. What do you call a cat that doesn't like to spend money?"

"A tight pussy."

17 just shook his head and chuckled. When they reached their separate posts, 17 looked back at 12. 12 smiled and nodded as if to say, "Oh c'mon. That's clever and you know it." 17 just chuckled and shook his head again and continued to scan the room.

Armory-43 was where the company stored various weapons. Items stored there would go to fund armies and militias of varying political and religious motivations. Elkhart Global Dynamics took no moral stance in conflicts and would trade freely with all sides. "We supply all groups equally, regardless of their views," they'd been told at orientation. The only real battle was who could keep paying longer. Thanks to Elkhart Global Dynamics, most world conflicts became more about whose well ran deeper. The bigger the bank account, the bigger the guns. It was simple as that.

Other armories contained weapons that were considerably more advanced than anything they actually distributed to even their highest investors. Elkhart's own personal weapons cache was years ahead of anything else. This would always ensure that Elkhart would have one up on the rest of the world.

Armory-43 was not part of Elkhart Global's personal cache, but it contained some of the more powerful weapons they sold. It was a large facility and heavily guarded. It was in this area that 12 and 17 had been posted that evening. Steel columns had been encased in plaster "to give a warmer feeling." Research had shown sterile looking steel walls drove down morale among employees.

At around 0100 hours the wall was blown asunder with a "Krakow!" 12 could only hear a piercing whistle and could only see a flash of white. White flash, white noise. Number 12 fumbled his way behind some crates. He prayed, in his own way, that the boxes he crawled behind contained no form of explosives. After several moments he regained his eyesight and saw panic around the armory. His hearing came back to find the sounds of gunfire. Other guards were running around firing at two or three heavily armed figures wearing trench coats. Based on his training he pieced together that these were probably members of the resistance movement B.A.T. (Brotherhood Against Tyranny). Blow in through the wall and come in guns blazing and balls to the wall. This was definitely their M.O.

"You okay, 17?" he cried out.

"Only physically," 17 called back.

12 saw a man with his back to a column on the other side of the room. The man dropped his two guns and drew two fresh Uzis from his jacket. Number 12 aimed his gun at him and shot off several rounds. The man was hit, but not killed, and ducked behind the column.

"Fuck," 12 muttered. "Hey! You still with me?"

"Oh yeah," said 17. "Pinned down though." Bullets were tearing up the sides of the boxes 17 had hidden behind.

"I'll draw their fire; you take 'em out."

"Okay!"

12 reloaded. "Count of three?"

"Yeah."

"One... two... ," 12 took a deep breath, "three."

He popped up and fired wildly. 17 stood up too and began firing. His gun took chunks out of the column. Bullets flew by 12's ears and he got back down, so he didn't see the grenade get tossed toward 17. All he heard was the blast.

"Ah, fuck!" 12 stood up, let loose a few more rounds, and lit up the trench coat-wearing cocksucker like the goddamn Fourth of July. Now no longer under fire, he ran over to his fallen comrade. He slipped on the blood and fell to the ground. He crawled over to Number 17 and clutched him in his arms.

"Fuck, man," 17 moaned. "I'm all fucked up."

"It's not that bad," 12 said.

"I'm fucked. Urg, that... fuck! I'm fucking... dying."

"Shut up with that shit. You're not fucking dying, okay?"

17 began to blubber, "Momma... momma..."

"Shh... hang in there, champ. We'll get you to the infirmary."

"I-I can't feel my legs."

"They're pinned under this crate," 12 said. 12 moved the crate, only to reveal entrails and no legs. He froze for a moment.

"There, it's fine," 12 lied. "Feel better?"

"Y-yeah," 17 sniffed, "but it still hurts a lot. I want my mom..."

"You're so brave, kiddo. Hang in there."

"C-could you give me something for the p-pain?" 17 could barely say.

"Yeah, buddy. I got my medical kit," 12 said as he drew his pistol from his boot. "I'll give you something for the pain."

17 managed to cough out something that sounded like, "Okay."

Tears welled up and Number 12 closed his eyes as he kissed his friend's forehead. 12 pressed the barrel of his standard issue sidearm into the back off his friend's head.

It went "Pop."

14/ SABOTAGE

"I've always prided myself on my judgement of character."
–Damien Elkhart

Number 9 and Number 3 walked down the hallway toward the central control room. Number 3's mind raced. She knew what she had to do, but she didn't know if she could do it. The night before she'd met with Liam Adams, who broke down the plan.

"Kat," he'd said, "we need you on this one."

"I... I don't know, Liam," she stuttered.

"You know better than anyone how unstable that man is! You said yourself he..."

"I know, Liam! I know what I fucking said, okay? That's not the problem."

"What is the problem?"

Number 9 looked at her friend. "Something wrong?"

"What?" 3 said, snapping out of her flashback.

"I said is something wrong?"

There was a pause. "No. No it's nothing."

"T-Minus three minutes!" the intercom announced. "Everyone to their positions."

The girls entered the control room. Number 3 was squirming with anticipation.

"If that satellite launches," she heard Liam say.

"It won't launch."

"You sure you can stop it on your own?"

"Yes."

"Mind if I ask how?"

"I'd prefer it if you didn't."

"Okay, Luv. Have it your way."

"Just make sure you're there to extract me in time. I'll take care of everything."

The satellite would allow Elkhart to send damaging broadcasts that would manipulate and destroy global communication. Only Elkhart Global Dynamics would have communication capabilities. Not only would it halt the spreading of false truths, it provided a very useful ultimatum: either people used Elkhart's services, or they didn't communicate at all. If anyone refused the conditions, well then they would be unable to call for help. To date it had been Elkhart's greatest undertaking. And it was about to be brought to fruition.

"T-minus two minutes," crackled over the loudspeaker as the girls took their seats. The control room looked into the center of the underground silo. Damien stood in the middle of the room with arms folded and smiling broadly.

"Glad you could join us, girls," he said

"Of course!" beamed Number 9.

"I wouldn't miss it for the world," said Number 3, taking her seat as she scanned the room. She felt for the gun strapped below her seat. It was about the size of a sawed-off shot gun. But it was a weapon designed to launch small explosives that would stick to the target. Its main purpose was for blowing up walls, doors, and small to medium vehicles.

"This is for the world," he said, kissing her on the cheek. She fought the urge to pull away. But it was apparent in her face she wanted to. He pressed his forehead to hers and added, "So glad you returned to my arms."

"T-minus one minute!" Damien Elkhart spun around and held out his arms. "The time is nigh, my children!" he proclaimed. "With this auspicious occasion we shall spread Truth to all the world's people. They will finally see what I have known!"

She had four targets. 1) The circuit board for the launch controls. 2) The thick window. 3) The satellite on the rocket. 4) Number 122, the man who designed it. She had already downloaded a virus into the satellite's files. Attempting to open them would fry the entire company's hard drive and trace and destroy all back up files.

"Thirty seconds left!"

The rest was in slow motion, and the volume on everything was turned down. She pulled the gun off the bottom of the seat. She stood up and began to fire. Her first shot hit the circuit board. The shell flew into the air, and the bomb stuck into the console. Sparks shot out and as she fired the second shot it burst, shooting fire and sparks across the room with debris. The second shot hit the window. Damien stood frozen in horror. Number 9 cried out, "Kat!?!"

The third shot went right into the back of Number 122. The window blew apart and the glass collapsed. She ran for the window as she fired the last shot into the side of the satellite. Just then Liam Adams appeared in the window wearing a harness, and she was tackled from the side. There was Lucy, gun drawn, tears filling her eyes.

"You, Kat!?!" she shrieked. "You!?!"

"Lucy, I didn't mean to hurt you."

"This matters to me, Kat! You betrayed us! You're betraying everything! How could you ruin this?"

Kathy swatted the gun from her friend's hand and slapped her. "Wake up, Lucy!" She ran and jumped into Liam Adams, who caught her and shouted, "Go! Go! Go!" They were air-lifted out and the satellite blew and Damien could barely be heard screaming, "Adams!"

Lucy could only stand in shock as the lights went out. Bulbs exploded, and the fire extinguishers sprayed down the room. She held her cheek. She fell to her knees and screamed. She punched the ground over and over, even after her hands began to bleed.

15/ THE FACELESS MAN FROM HUMAN RESOURCES

"A man cannot lose himself in his work. He is his work."
–Damien Elkhart

Out of the kindness of their hearts, Elkhart Global Dynamics held a funeral of sorts for those who had fallen that week. Number 12 was in attendance for 17's ceremony. He sat in the back and did not speak. The ceremony consisted of the Faceless Man from Human Resources listing off his accomplishments and discussing the amount of time spent with the company. They also would present the compensation to the families in a ceremonial fashion. This was an idea cooked up by the Public Relations department.

"We should not think of Number 17 as being gone," faceless H.R. man said. "Number 17 has just left to pursue other metaphysical interests..."

Number 17's only listed next of kin was his nineteen-year-old sister, Sarah, who had on more than one occasion touched Number 12's penis. This was not to Number 17's knowledge. Sarah called 12 "T.K." She called 17 "Karl." Sarah was presented the money and she cried. Damien Elkhart himself placed his hand on her shoulder and thanked her for "giving up her loved one for the Truth." She thanked him despite his words meaning nothing to her.

Number 12 had the day off. He found Sarah outside and she threw her arms around him and buried her face into his chest. They went back to her house and let loose their collective mourning in an act of tear-filled sex. Tyler lay on the couch and Sarah's tears rolled down as she kissed his face and bounced, twisted, and ground out her grief. Tyler never cried during sex. But this time he could not help himself. He had been trying to hold it back. But hearing Sarah sniffle as she kissed his neck for some reason made him lose it. Once she saw he was crying too, she threw herself on him more and they fell into each other.

The Faceless Man from Human Resources had no face; quite literally. He had a mouth and eyes. His nose was little more than a pair of nostrils. But anything that might be considered a distinguishing characteristic was suspiciously absent. No one knew what was up with that. The word on the bathroom wall was that he was "a primie" born before such things could fully develop. Another such rumor is that all distinguishing characteristics were burned off in an accident. Some said that he'd been horribly burned and fallen into a coma, making reconstructive surgery far too risky. When he came to some months later, all his facial characteristics were gone, and nothing could be done to restore them.

But the truth of the matter, Tyler told Sarah, was that his face had merely faded over the years. It was a phenomenon that left doctors and clergymen alike baffled. He once had an entire face, back when he first started. He'd even had a family and enjoyed fishing on weekends. The more the years passed, the more focused on his job he became, the more those things faded from his life.

Back when the Faceless Man from H.R. had a face, he and his wife, Karen, had three children: two handsome sons of 7 and 13, and a 12-year-old daughter. They had not made love since the conception of their youngest son, Aaron. Karen's constant accusations of, "You're fucking someone else," were, of course, unfounded.

"I am not," he would say in a dry tone without looking up from the work he'd brought home with him. "What makes you think that?"

Her point that he was "certainly not fucking her," although true, proved nothing. He'd simply lost interest in all things sexual. It just simply wasn't productive. Time spent fucking was time spent not working, and he had too much work to do. He had no time for recreation. He'd even stopped fishing on weekends.

On the day of one of his larger promotions, he came home to find his family dressed nicely and ready to go out to celebrate.

"Where are you all going?" he asked in his increasingly hollow tone.

"We thought we'd go to a nice restaurant and celebrate your promotion," his wife explained, eager to dress nice and go out into the world with her family, which they had not done in ages.

"Don't be ridiculous," he'd said. "I just got promoted today and I have work to do. I cannot slack off right after being promoted."

The kids just stared at their mother, whose eye was twitching and their father went into his office. She burst in the door and said, "You just fucking got home from work."

He looked over the reports he had e-mailed to himself. "Hmm?"

"I said 'You just. Fucking got home. From fucking work."

"Language," he reminded her.

"Do you know how long it's been since we've been out as a family? Hell, how long it's been since the two of us went out? Since we've made love?"

"I can try and pencil in..."

"Did you even know that Aaron's grades are in the toilet? Do you even care? You used to help him study. Shaun, that's our oldest..."

"I know who Shaun is."

"Well, I felt I had to make sure. Shaun was chosen as the MVP of his Little League team. Our daughter, Sue. She had her period. Did you know that?"

"Sue had her period this week?" he asked for confirmation.

"Sue had her period six months ago!" his wife yelled. She slammed the door behind her and took the kids out to dinner and a movie. He turned back to his work.

The next day he returned home to find a note and an empty house. Several days later the divorce papers were served. He filed his copy and turned back to his work. His face had already started to fade.

That was Tyler's version, at least.

16/ SARAH JENSON

"If you want to bring people together, make them experience tragedy together."
–Damien Elkhart

Tyler lay naked next to Sarah. It was a warm night and she did not have air-conditioning and so they'd slept on top of the covers. He looked at the clock and sighed, knowing that in only a few hours he would be back on the clock and doing others' bidding as Number 12. Sarah stirred and he looked at her and she kissed him. Without his asking she relieved his morning wood with a blow job. It didn't last long and didn't feel that great when he came. In fact it left him with a groggy feeling in the pit of his stomach. Tyler hated mornings. He sat up and swung his legs over the side of the bed.

"How're you holding up?" He asked.

"I dunno," she said. "I miss him."

Tyler concurred simply by nodding.

"How're you?" she asked, stroking his back. There was a pause as he searched for an answer. He didn't find one, so he said nothing.

He picked his underwear up off the floor and slid into them, then his pants.

"Where are you going?" Sarah asked.

"Home. I gotta shower before I go in."

"Just shower here," Sarah suggested. She sat up and wrapped her arms around his neck from behind pressing her still bare breasts against his back. She slid her hand down to his crotch. "I can lather you up..."

"That's a sweet thought," he said, gently pushing her off, "But I've gotta change anyway."

She slumped back onto the bed Indian style and crossed her arms and pouted. "Fine," she said.

He slipped his arms into his shirt. "Look," he said as he pulled his white t-shirt over his head, "I want you to know that just because of this... you don't have to stop seeing other people..."

"You're very funny," she said.

"So I'm told," he said and gave her a peck. "Call you?"

"Sure, T.K.," Sarah said. "That'd be great."

"Maybe grab a beer tonight if I don't get off too late?"

"Tonight's no good," she said. "I have a date."

"Oh," he said, "some other time then."

"Some other time," she slowly repeated, looking away.

"Later," he said, and was off.

Tyler tested the water pouring out of the faucet before he pulled up the pin to start the shower. He stuck his head under the flow of water so that it hit him on the back where his head met his neck. He splashed warm water into his face to help wash away that feeling of grogginess. "Degroggification" was the word he and Karl had made up to describe the process.

He thought about Sarah and remembered her saying she had a date later that evening. He heaved a heavy sigh. Tyler Kelly was not a religious man. Still, with the wet tip of his finger, he began to draw crosses on the dry mortar between the tiles on the shower wall. He stared at them a moment and with a hand full of water, splashed them all away, then punched the tiles, cracking some of the older ones. His mind wandered as the water splashed on his head.

Tyler shut off the shower. The nozzles squeaked. He opened the sliding glass door and blindly felt around for his towel. He dried off and stared at the mail on his coffee table. The discrepancy between his paycheck and loan bills brought only sighs and a need to sip from the warm, half-empty beer on the side table. He got dressed and went back to work.

Since the loss of her brother, Sarah Jenson was pretty much alone in the world. Karl had been the only family she had for the last five years, and he too was now gone.

Karl's life insurance had paid off double, which provided Sarah more than enough to cover her tuition and cost of living for a couple of years. She really did have a date the evening following her night with T.K. This was something she'd had planned for a number of days. Ron, a boy from her anthropology class, had asked her for her number one night at the campus bar. She had accepted, not only because Ron had nice pecs but also because it might provide her a chance to feel something, the same thing that had led her into Tyler's arms. Tyler and Sarah made love three times and she'd come twice. It was not her first time. She'd lost her virginity at sixteen, but it was her first time having an orgasm. Maybe it was the emotion or maybe Tyler did something the others hadn't. Either way it was the first time she realized what the fuss was all about.

Ron picked Sarah up around 8 p.m. He hugged her before she was ready and offered his condolences for her loss.

"Thanks," she said.

"Are you sure you're ready to go out?" he asked.

"I just need to get out," she said. He took her to a dance club, the line outside wrapped around the corner.

"Are we even going to be able to get in?" Sarah asked, not really caring whether or not they could.

"Sure," said Ron. "Follow me." He took her to the back alley, where there was another bouncer by the side door.

"Heya, Ron," the bouncer said, letting them in.

Ron performed an elaborate handshake with the bouncer. "Johnny boy!" he said. Johnny boy let them in.

"How'd you get us in?" she asked.

"My fraternity runs the place," he said.

She feigned being impressed and they took their seats.

"Do you want a drink?" he asked her.

"Oh my God, yes," she said.

"Let me guess," he said, "Cran-Vodka?"

She had really wanted a Scotch and soda, but instead she decided to make Ron feel like he was showing her a good time.

"Yes," she said. "How did you know?"

"I just had a feeling," he smiled and went to order their drinks. Normally Sarah would think to herself how stereotypical that was. He only made that assumption because so many girls her age ordered Cran-Vodkas. But her mind didn't even wander there at all. It was on the closed casket. Tyler had been the one to tell her. He'd left work right afterward and came to her door early in the morning. He was standing in the breaking light of dawn, shaking, and could not look at her at first. Her heart sank at the sight.

"He's gone, Sarah," he said, finally looking at her. "I'm so sorry. I'm so fucking sorry." Not saying anything she threw her arms around him. They stood like this for several minutes. She sobbed and he stroked her back.

Ron was saying something.

"What?" said Sarah.

"I said, 'Here's your drink.'"

"Oh, sorry," she took the drink and slammed it back. The cranberry juice made it go down too easily. "'nother?" she asked.

"Uh, sure," he said. When he returned he brought back several.

Tyler had told her everything, even how he'd had to put Karl out of his misery.

"I couldn't stand to see him suffer. Karl deserved more than to go out in that much pain."

Only a small part of Sarah blamed Tyler for what had happened. But she knew by looking at Tyler that it had to be done. And she knew how hard it must have been for Tyler to be the one to make the call. She kissed his forehead.

"Thank you," she'd said. "On behalf of Karl, thank you."

"I thought you should hear it from me. I rushed over so I could get here before they called you."

She just held him and they fell asleep on the couch. After about forty-five minutes of dozing, Elkhart Global's H.R. department called. It was a prerecorded message.

"We regret to inform you about the loss of your loved one. Since this tragedy occurred while on the clock, the insurance provided will be substantial. We realize that the financial benefits are no compensation for your loss and offer our sincerest condolences. Please call our offices between the hours of 8am and 4pm Monday through Thursday or 9am-12pm Friday for information on how to proceed with this matter."

"You're really pounding those back," said Ron. At this point Sarah was very intoxicated but feeling no better about anything.

"I just... ," she said.

"Just what?"

"I just need to feel something other than this, y'know?" she said.

"I understand," he said. "Let's go back to your place and I'll help you take your mind off it."

When they got home Ron kissed her aggressively. She undid his belt as they headed for the bedroom. Once there he pulled her dress up over her head and threw her onto the bed. They fucked. Sarah did not come.

17/ EXPERIMENT

"Damaged people are able to be rebuilt. Molded.
They are more willing to accept the Truth."
–Damien Elkhart

Number 9 was conducting another of her experiments on the fourteenth floor. Number 12 was feeling her up in a broom closet. They were both on their break, and she'd brushed past him, "accidentally" rubbing her breast against his arm. He turned around and saw her enter the broom closet; she stroked the edge of the door frame as she closed the door behind her. He followed. Without saying a word she grabbed his collar and thrust her mouth against his. He'd begun by stroking her sides, but she grabbed his hand and moved it to her breast. She used her hand to guide his in the rhythm she wanted. Once he got it she moved her hand to his belt buckle, undid it, and began to rub his moderately sized erection through his underpants. This went on for the full half hour. When break was up she left first. He remained for several moments before leaving himself. At no point did either one say a word.

She'd seen Number 12 spending a great deal of time with Number 17 before 17 had died. They would carry on during lunch and break times. They played well off each other. During missions and guard detail, they were virtually unstoppable. They seemed to share a connection normally set aside for twins. The two men made a hell of a team. Watching those two reminded Number 9 of Number 3. The memories saddened her, so she turned her attention back to the young man kissing her neck. She grabbed his waist and adjusted herself so his leg rested between hers. She grew slightly flush at the feeling of his leg rubbing against her special place, and the memories washed away, if only momentarily.

Number 23 sat at a computer console with data reflected on his glasses. He scrolled through information at Herculean rates, absorbing as much as he could. He was confident in his hacking abilities and had only been getting better at it ever since his moral outlook had changed. Such a sin came naturally to him. So how could it be a sin at all?

The operation he was assigned to, unlike his digression to South American temples, was well within his realm of skill and interest. This stage of the plan was, in truth, rather elementary; but God's mercy on anyone who tried to tell Damien Elkhart this. The plan would have been in the early chapters of any aspiring revolutionary guidebook: Tamper with the water supply. Number 23's part was to hack into the water treatment facility and shut down the security systems. He was also required to shut down the chemical purifiers long enough for the team to add their own little concoction.

This drug, which was developed and personally tested by Damien Elkhart himself, was named "Truth" by its creator. Truth had already hit the streets and had gained the slang name "Capital T." Capital T was put out on the streets in earlier phases to determine whether or not it would garner the desired results. After several months in circulation, it proved itself and a strain was finalized. Capital T was the fruit of many labors, including (but not limited to) the numerous raids on and the absorption of several pharmaceutical companies.

The time, however, was not yet right to unleash it unto the masses. Damien Elkhart needed time to develop more of a following so that when people partook of and saw Truth, it would be to him that they turned.

18/ THE REVIEW BOARD

"He who can't answer for himself must be questioned."
–Damien Elkhart

When Tyler Kelly arrived at work the day after sleeping with Sarah Jenson, he was stopped by his supervisor, the jittery Number 92.

"12," he said, "You're up for review. The board wants to see you as soon as you clock in."

"I was just about to."

"Well, the review board wants to see you," 92 said yet again.

"Okay."

"Just go see them after you clock in. Room 57."

Number 12 rolled his eyes. "Alright." He slid his card through the clock and it went "Bah-tweet."

The door to Room 57 opened and Number 12 poked his head in. There was a long table of a half-dozen men in suits sitting on the same side. Their chairs looked expensive and each had a handle to control the chair on the right arm. Most of their faces were obscured by shadow, as the one side of the table was dimly lit.

"Have a seat," he was told by all of the men in unison. One man wheeled his chair forward. He was a man in his mid-thirties, dark haired and clean shaven. He was pale white with green eyes. He motioned towards a folding chair in front of the table under the light. Number 12 sat down, squinting slightly.

"Do you know what this review is in regards to?" he was asked by the man who had wheeled forward.

"The assault on Armory-43," another man explained.

"I was on guard detail that night. It was The B.A.T. It matched their M.O. and it was their uniforms."

"We are aware of that," said one. "We have not called you in as a witness," said another.

There was an awkward pause.

"What is this about then?"

"Number 17," said a member of the board who had not spoken up yet.

Number 12 did not say anything but he could not hide the reaction on his face.

"Does this make you uncomfortable, Number... ," he paused as he checked the files.

"12," said another man. Number 12 could only look down and around trying to hide the welling of tears in his eyes.

"I'll ask you again," they all said, "Does this..."

"Yes! Fuck! It makes me uncomfortable!" he blurted.

"Do you care to comment on the trajectory of the bullet wound in Number 17's head?"

"Is that what this is about?" Number 12 asked.

"So you do freely admit that you..."

"Killed him? Yes. I did. But..."

"... killed him."

"He was dying. Suffering. His intestines were..."

"This is not a murder trial," they explained. All of them wheeled forward. They were all dark haired, pale white, green eyed, mid-thirties. They looked like clones of one another.

"What the fu--,"

"You wasted company resources. This review is an official warning for the misappropriation of supplies."

"What supplies? Are you blaming me for the destroyed merchandise? I was just a guard. Are you calling all of us in on this? Because we failed to..."

"We will ask the questions here."

"You wasted your ammunition, a company resource..."

"The bullet?" Number 12 laughed. Not because he found it funny, but only because he did not know what else to do. "You've gotta be shitting me."

"You wasted a bullet on a dead man."

"I didn't want him to die in pain, okay? Do you get that? He was—"

"The misuse of company resources is highly frowned upon. It

is inefficient and in contradiction to the Elkhart Ideal. Article Four, Paragraph Two on page One-Hundred-Twenty-Seven of your employee handbook specifically states that the use of ammunition as a means of euthanasia is considered misuse of company property and is means for a disciplinary review."

Number 12 just sighed.

"Now, Number 12, you have proven yourself in a number of ways in your short time here. It has been interesting to watch you grow in the company. In light of your services, we are letting you off with a verbal warning. Now..." he slid forward a sheet of paper, "Please sign this form stating that you have met with us and will improve your performance in the future."

Number 12 leaned forward, signed the sheet. He pressed down so hard he tore the paper. He sat up and left the room, slamming the door behind him. He did not hear them thank him for his time.

19/ PROPHETIC DREAMS

"Truth is shown when our filters are off. In sleep, I have seen things."
–Damien Elkhart

One evening 12 was witness to obligatory banter between two rivals. Damien Elkhart had captured one of his arch-nemeses, a suave and stylish man whose exact loyalties were unknown. What was known about him was that he'd worked as a spy for both the United States and the United Kingdom. His name was Liam Adams and he'd be a thorn in the side of Elkhart for a number of years. Adams had been captured and was strapped to a medieval torture device. Large wheels were hooked to other large wheels, which when turned would stretch out his limbs.

"Tell me, Liam. Have you ever had a prophetic dream?" Damien Elkhart asked with his back to Liam Adams.

"Like a dream that came true?" Liam asked.

"Yes. Like a dream that came true. Precisely," said Damien.

"Well, once I dreamt that my father died. The dream felt so real..."

"And that's when your father died?" Mr. Elkhart asked.

"No, he was fine. Our milkman dropped dead on our porch the next day though."

"Very amusing, Liam..."

"I thought so."

"You just never take anything seriously, Liam," Damien scolded. "You have the naïve arrogance of a child, and that is why you will always be blind to the Truth!"

"I'm sorry. What? I wasn't paying attention..."

"You know you're only amusing yourself, Liam."

"Just keeping things interesting, Elky-Poo."

"I've always had an interest in history," Elkhart said. "I got this little device after I purchased the British Museum. It still works. It did take some touching up. A few parts needed to be rebuilt. But, still, they don't make them like this anymore."

"What exactly do you think you'll accomplish, Elkhart?"

"You should know that by now, my dear Liam. We've done this so many times before."

"You mean where you babble out some damn word soup? Every time you open your mouth, it's just a total mind fuck."

"I fuck minds alright. I fuck minds with ideas and impregnate them with thoughts to produce a child known as 'The Truth!'"

"See, that's what I'm talking about. That doesn't mean a goddamn thing."

"I've heard enough blasphemy from you, Liam," Damien Elkhart cranked the device's wheels and stretched out Liam Adams who grunted in pain. Elkhart held out his hand, "Knife!"

Number 235 handed Mr. Elkhart a twisted looking blade. "These were used in Ancient Egypt in the mummification process."

Liam Adams laughed through the pain, "Always knew you were a mummyfucker..."

Before anyone could react the following happened:

Damien Elkhart thrust the blade downward; Liam Adams reached up with his left hand and knocked the blade out of his hand. The cut rope fell to the ground. Before the guards could aim their guns, Liam Adams had Elkhart and was holding a blade to his throat. The blade extended from his watch.

"Together again, eh, Elky?" Liam whispered into his ear. 12 cocked his gun.

"Easy, cowboy..." Liam said. 12 backed off.

"It's amazing what people will do for their 401k, wouldn't you agree, Elky?"

"Someone kill this fuck!" Elkhart shrieked.

The guards approached and Liam backed towards the window.

"You're outnumbered, Adams," Elkhart said.

"Well then," Adams said, "Cheers!" He kicked Elkhart into the line of guards. Some fell down, a few caught him but were knocked back.

Adams had slipped out the window and was gone.

Elkhart stood up. "Argh! Who is responsible for this?!" The henchmen stood around, confused. "Who tied him up? C'mon! Who?"

Number 93 stepped forward apprehensively.

"Why... didn't you take the watch?"

"Wh-what?"

"The watch. Why didn't you remove it?"

"It was... jus-just a watch?"

"It is not just a watch! It's never just a watch!" Elkhart screamed.

Elkhart grabbed Number 93 by the neck and threw him to the ground. "Failure will not be tolerated...," Damien Elkhart looked over the rest of the men. "You," he pointed at 12, "Kill him." He pointed at 93. 12 sighed and rolled his eyes.

Damien Elkhart walked out of the room.

"Failure will never be tolerated."

The gunshot echoed down the hall.

20/ THE DUKES

"There's no 'T' in 'team.' But 'leader' also has an 'ea'.
So, you see, they're connected."
–Damien Elkhart

Elkhart had done right in recruiting Kenny D to be Number 45. His street smarts and past leadership experience made him the perfect candidate to lead a small group on some of the more crucial operations. As a matter of fact, he'd found some of the members of his team were former members of his gang, The Dukes, whom he had not seen since their respective arrests.

There was B. Dawg, who was now an expert at demolitions and called Number 54. Car Jack was now an even better driver than when he ran with The Dukes. He was called 33. Also joining the group was Swoll Tim, still muscular and always ready for a fight. Swoll Tim now went by 52. And ever since Cooper X learned to not hold his gun sideways, he was a crack shot. He received no end of ribbing for the fact he'd been assigned Number 69. There were a number of others in 45's unit; however, they were often killed off or used in an expendable manner.

"Liam Adams has been sticking his nose where it doesn't belong again," Damien Elkhart told 45. "I'd very much like to have a chat with him. Bring him to me. Alive."

Number 45's mind was already working out a plan. Liam Adams was notoriously difficult to apprehend and apparently even more difficult to keep captive. But the latter was someone else's problem. He figured the best way was to lure Adams to him somehow. Perhaps capture someone close to Adams? No, his guard would be up. Besides, who was Adams close to anyway? It'd never work. He'd lose people, and that meant paperwork. He hated paperwork. No, the best idea would be to distract Adams with something, throw him off his guard. An explosion would do the trick. 54 could handle that. He would have to find some way to close off escape routes and limit it to one that Adams would be forced to take; then they'd be there waiting. Number 69 could use gunfire to steer Adams in a certain direction if need be.

45 had one of his lesser team members gather some intelligence regarding Adams's usual M.O. It turned out the newbie was very adept at research and was able to hack into the tracking system of the organization Adams worked for. They had him.

The key was to create an explosion that would cause convincing enough damage, but would allow Adams to get away alive so he could be apprehended.

The plan was as follows: disguise a man as a delivery boy dropping off a package, which would be the bomb, follow Adams into a location...

The Dukes got into position and waited. They watched as their package boy left the building. They braced themselves. Several moments later Adams dove out of the second floor window in the alley and landed in the dumpster. Seconds later an explosion blew out the wall. When Adams poked his head out of the dumpster, Number 45 was standing there with a gun to Adams's head. 45 grinned.

Five others had assault rifles pointed at him. Adams put his hands behind his head, and the muscular Number 52 pulled him out of the dumpster and patted him down, removing all concealed weapons.

They brought Adams to Damien Elkhart and shoved him forward. Adams stumbled but maintained his balance with an ever-present grace. 12 grabbed Adams by the collar of his shirt.

"Liam..." said Damien.

"Damien..." said Liam.

"A job well done, gentlemen. You may leave us now."

As the Dukes left the room, Number 45 passed by 12. The two caught each others' eyes. 12 recognized 45 but could not place him. 45 mouthed "What?" then turned and exited.

Damien Elkhart summoned forth Number 93.

"You," Damien said, "Show Mr. Adams here to... the device..."

"Yes, sir," said 93.

"You've been sticking your nose where it doesn't belong, Mr. Adams. You have a bad habit of that."

"I also have a habit of sticking my dick into your mother," Adams retorted.

"Liam, Liam, Liam," Damien sighed. "How can a man so poised and eloquent be so... vulgar?"

"Rest assured, my dear Elky, it's a side I show only to you."

"I'm honored," Elkhart said with dark sarcasm.

Number 93 tied the ropes tight around Liam Adams's wrists.

"Nice watch," 93 said.

"Thanks," said Adams.

21/ CRAN VODKA

*"Those imbued with the creator seize control in a
world where people love to lose it."*
–Damien Elkhart

Tyler Kelly's alcohol consumption had increased steadily since the
demise of Karl Jenson. He sat at the bar of The Capitol and signaled the
bartender for yet another bourbon with a beer chaser.

"So," said the gentleman next to him, "what do you do for a living?"

"Who? Me?" Tyler asked.

"Yeah," said the man, "you."

"I'm a henchman," Tyler said.

The man nodded and sipped his drink. "I did that for a while. Still
have some friends in it. Who do you hench for?"

"Elkhart Global Dynamics," Tyler said, "just across the road."

"Damien Elkhart, eh? That the one that fancies himself the new
Messiah?"

"Yeah, that'd be the one," Tyler said nonchalantly.

"You think he's got what it takes?" The man asked.

"What do you mean?" Tyler asked.

"A lot come and go," said the man, "but few truly make a mark. And
I've yet to see one truly succeed. But there's a lot of buzz about Elkhart."

"I guess," said Tyler. "So, what do you do now?"

"Investment banking," he said. "Nothing exciting. But it pays the
mortgage. And keeps the wife happy," he added.

"That's always important," Tyler said.

"Yes it is, my young friend. Yes it is."

"I'm gonna step outside for a cigarette," Tyler said.

"Be my guest. I should get back to the Mrs., speaking of 'er. Night."

Tyler stepped outside, buzzing immensely as he lit himself a Lucky
Strike. Sarah Jenson pulled up and smiled when she saw him.

"T.K.," she said, "I didn't know you smoked."

"I didn't use to," he said. "I can put it out if you want me to."

Sarah smiled at him and took the cigarette out of his hand and took a drag. "You should light another one," she said, keeping it. Tyler lit a new one for himself.

"It's nice to actually see you again," Tyler said.

Sarah looked down at her feet and then away. "Don't fucking say that shit to me, Tyler."

"Don't fucking say what shit to you?" Tyler said with an air of annoyance. "It is, is all."

"Yeah, well…" She tossed the cigarette down and stomped on it. Without saying anything else, she threw the door open and went inside the bar. Both of them were hurt by her comment, though neither could say where it had come from.

Tyler flicked his cigarette. The Lucky Strike struck the ground and the cherry burst, shooting orange sparks on the blacktop like an exploding transformer. Tyler stumbled slightly as he lit another and searched for his car. Since he had started henching for Elkhart, Tyler Kelly had killed thirteen men, including his best friend. A baker's dozen. He plopped into the seat of his car and rolled down the windows. He turned on the stereo and caught himself in the rear-view mirror before backing out of the space and driving off to who-gives-a-shit-where.

Sarah sat down at the bar and ordered a cran-vodka (just a touch of the cran). She looked back at the door, expecting Tyler to follow her in. When he didn't, she felt a confusing mixture of relief and disappointment. As painful and awkward as spending time with him had become, she couldn't help but want to, though she would never, could never, admit it to Tyler. She figured it was best that he didn't follow her. She was actually here to meet Ron, the boy from her class she'd started seeing. It would have been awkward, especially since she hadn't told Tyler she was seeing anybody officially.

Sarah saw Ron enter The Capitol Bar & Grill, peeking over the heads, looking for her. She smiled and waved to him. He acknowledged her with a nod and a smile that showed the top row of his teeth. Ron put his arm around Sarah and kissed her on the cheek before taking a seat on the stool next to her.

"Hey, baby," he said to her. "Rolling Rock," he said to the bartender.

"It's good to see you," she said.

"It's nice to see you too," he said. Then he added, "How are you?"

"Okay, I 'spose," she said. "The insurance money from Karl has been covering my living expenses, but I'm not going to have enough to cover tuition next semester."

"What are you going to do?" Ron asked.

"Work," she said as she gazed into the red drink. "A lot."

"A friend of mine might be hiring," Ron offered. "I can talk to him."

"No," Sarah said, "you don't have to do that."

He smiled, then kissed her on the cheek. "I insist."

"That's really sweet of you, Ron," she said, "but you shouldn't feel you have to."

"It's not a bother if you want me to talk to him," he said.

"Do what you want," Sarah said flatly but without sarcasm.

"Expect a phone call tomorrow," Ron said. "Sometime in the afternoon?"

"Okay," she smiled at him a little.

He smiled back. "Okay." This was followed by several moments of awkward silence. Ron had ordered and drunk most of his second Rolling Rock before asking.

"Talk to Tyler lately?"

"I don't really want to talk about Tyler," she said.

"Why not?" Ron asked. "I mean, he's your friend right? He sounds like a cool guy."

"He is," she said, "But..."

"But... ?" said Ron.

She chewed on the end of her straw and put it back into her drink, pushing it down into the bottom of the glass until in bent at a 90-degree angle. "Nothing," she said. "Don't worry about it."

"Alright," he said. "I won't."

But Ron worried a little bit. It didn't take someone with extra sensory perception to pick up on the sexual tension between the two. He hadn't even met Tyler, but just from the way Sarah talked about Tyler Ron knew something had happened there, and he was sweating a little at the possibility of something happening again. He cleared his throat and shifted his weight on the stool. They both finished their drinks without saying a word to the other.

"It's complicated," she said finally.

"Hmm?" said Ron in a vain attempt to pretend he'd forgotten what they were talking about.

"Tyler," she said. "He and Karl were like best friends. And when he died..." she trailed off, then simply shrugged.

"When he died..." Ron gestured for her to continue. She opened her mouth to speak but at the last moment she merely paused.

"I don't want to talk about it," she said quickly, then took a sip.

"Of course not," he said, or rather muttered, to himself.

"What was that?" she said, looking at him.

"Nothing," he said.

"Look, we were grieving together and in a moment of weakness... something happened. But it was before you and I were really going out. So just let it go, okay? Don't worry about it."

"Wait. What do you mean before we were *really* going out?" he said.

"I mean you and I weren't going out when it happened. That's what I said."

"No," Ron reminded her, "You said we weren't *really* going out when it happened."

"I mean, like, before we were officially steady," Sarah said.

"Oh I see," he said, noticeably hurt by the clarified information, "Fine. Okay. That's cool."

"Do you want to go?" she asked.

"Fine. Sure. Whatever." He paid for the drinks. They walked out and she took his hand. Somewhat reluctantly he took hers and they walked back to his house. Sarah sat on Ron's bed and then lay back. She rubbed her eyes and yawned.

"Tired?" Ron asked.

"No. Just a little tipsy."

Ron walked over to a box on his dresser and opened it. He slid a pre-rolled joint out of a bag and lit it. He took a drag as he sat down next to her. He handed it to her as he slowly exhaled. She took it from him, touching his fingers, and inhaled deeply, as though she'd just run a seven-minute mile and was gasping for air. The smoke billowed out between her lips, and her mind wandered. She thought of Tyler. What he must be doing now. Hoping he wasn't doing anything too rash. She pictured him sitting in his apartment, watching bad movies and drinking whiskey straight from the bottle. She was right. Mostly. (Tyler was, in actuality, drinking rum.)

Buzzing on the booze and the weed Sarah, moved her hand towards Ron's zipper. She started with slow, easy strokes and when he was hard she used her mouth. He smiled, put one hand behind his head and took a hit off the joint.

22/ A PRISONER

"Jesus was called a blasphemer. I'm in good company."
–Damien Elkhart

A member of The B.A.T. stood unconscious with his arms tied above his head to a stake in the middle of a large arena-like space.

"Hit him," said Damien Elkhart.

12 stepped forward with a bucket of water and splashed the prisoner. The prisoner coughed and sputtered.

"Rise and shine," said Damien Elkhart.

"It's you," said the prisoner.

"Of course," said Damien Elkhart. "I wouldn't be anyone else."

The prisoner spit on him. "Fuck you, Elkhart."

"Well, despite your less-than-sober attitude, I've decided to bestow upon you a great honor. You will be testing our new weapon."

12 left the arena and stood in the wings to guard the entrance to the control room.

"Hello, 12," said Number 23 from the control panel.

"Hey, how's it going?"

"Oh, y'know. Same ol'..."

"I feel ya," Number 12 concurred.

"Would you listen to this person?" Number 23 pointed out to the middle of the arena. The man was yelling at Elkhart.

"You think you know what's best for everybody?" He yelled, "You arrogant fuck! You can't control people! You and your convoluted truth will rot in Hell!"

"Like he hasn't heard that one before," said 23, chuckling.

"It's almost as if life is on reruns," said 12. "I'm really feeling the monotony these days."

"Well, you'll get that with any job," Number 23 reminded him.

"You're probably right," Number 12 said.

Damien Elkhart walked away from the stake and made a circle with his hand above his head.

"There's the signal," said 23. He flipped a few switches and pulled back a lever. There was a whirring sound like pistons charging up. The two men put on ear muffs and protective eye wear.

"Hit it," said 12.

23 pushed a lit-up red button. The man screamed and there was a quick flash and a modest "Pop!" Where the man once stood was a smoking stain on the ground.

"It worked," said 23.

"Groovy. Lunch?" said 12.

"Lunch," said 23.

23/ OSCAR

"People need to feel saved. Give them something to be saved from."
—Damien Elkhart

Tyler Kelly slouched in his chair, feet propped up on the ottoman. He had fallen asleep there sometime between the hours of two and three in the morning. His cat, Oscar, leapt up onto his stomach around seven o'clock, waking Tyler.

"Oof!" Tyler grunted. Oscar crawled around Tyler and sat on Tyler's chest.

"Mrow!" said Oscar, who had recently been diagnosed with diabetes. Oscar didn't have much time left but wasn't showing any signs of discomfort. "Mrow!"

"Hey, old man," Tyler said to his cat. "Good morning to you, too."

"Mrow!" Oscar said, rubbing his head on the stubble that had formed on Tyler's chin. "Mrrrroooow!" Tyler rubbed Oscar's head. Oscar squinted and purred. The cat turned around and jumped off Tyler, kicking Tyler in the crotch.

"Dammit, Oscar!" Tyler yelled.

"Mrooooow!" moaned Oscar.

"Okay, okay," Tyler relented. "I'm up! I'm up. I'll feed you. I'll feed you."

Tyler had had Oscar for around 15 years. The cat had been a part of his life longer than most people. With Karl dead and Sarah blowing him off, all of a sudden Tyler was fast running out of friends. He gave Oscar fresh water and put food in his bowl.

"Mow," Oscar said, satisfied, and stuck his face into his bowl and began munching. Tyler checked his watch and decided to shower before work. He'd let himself ripen over the weekend and figured he might get an assignment today where a distinct stench would be detrimental.

In his old age Oscar no longer made cleaning himself a priority. His fur was beginning to get knotted and slightly greasy. Occasionally Tyler would wake up at 4 a.m. to a "Grrrr" and find Oscar on the floor beside his bed pulling the knots out with his mouth. Startled somewhat Tyler would throw on the light and look down to see Oscar toss a clump of hair to the side and then turn to him, squinting and purring.

Oscar munched at his food and Tyler sighed. He climbed into the shower and stroked down his morning wood. He lathered himself up and rinsed off, spending just enough time to get the grime off. Still wearing a towel, Tyler stepped outside and scooped up the newspaper. He unfolded it as he sat down to his breakfast of Cheerios and English muffins with butter and honey. The front page of the newspaper cried of a crisis at a major financial institution.

The world's financial state has been put in jeopardy after a hostage situation at an International Trade Exchange yesterday morning. Terrorists infiltrated at around 10:30. Various stock traders, major business owners, and some government accountants were among the hostages. No names have been released.

Explosive charges had been placed around the building. It is believed the terrorists were attempting to damage the world's economy by destroying the ITE and assassinating key economic strategists.

The charges were detonated at 12:14 pm after a failed police stand off. Several of the hostages were killed, and others were taken by the perpetrators. The names of the deceased have yet to be released.

Corporate Tycoon Damien Elkhart has offered financial and spiritual assistance to the victims of the tragedy.

Tyler stopped reading there. He poured a second cup of coffee and flipped open his phone. He stared at Sarah's name for a few moments before hitting 'dial.' She did not answer. He left no message.

In the locker room Number 12 was greeted with a photo of Sarah, Karl, and himself on the inside of his locker door. They were standing close together. Sarah had her arm around his waist, and he had Karl in a headlock and his other arm around Sarah's shoulder. All three were giving peace signs. He threw threw his bag on the floor of the locker, wandered past all of his half naked co-workers, and checked the bulletin board for the day's assignments. Above the bulletin board was a motivational poster announcing that you were right whether you thought you could or could not do something. Next to his number was a short coded entry. F27b. As per the routine he wandered over to a wall that looked like safe deposit boxes. He found the box with the corresponding code and slid his ID card through it. Recognizing he was authorized for the boxes, it made an obnoxious, piercing "Bleep" not unlike the one replacing swear words on basic cable. He took out the envelope with his name on it. The mission would involve hazardous materials and infiltration.

Number 12 headed back to his locker and pulled out the appropriate attire. A one-piece spandex underwear; a full body rubber suit, which truth be told was a bit uncomfortable, but he had gotten used to it; as well as a chest armor plate and a gas mask. Tyler put the spandex hood over his head and tucked his hair underneath before putting on the head wear for the rubber haz mat suit. He tucked the gas mask and helmet under his arm and headed to the briefing room. He took a chair toward the back; everyone else began to pour into the room.

"You, in the back," the man giving the briefing said to 12 (though he couldn't remember his number; they'd only met once before), "why don't you join us? Move up a few rows."

Number 12 heaved a sigh more heavily than he had intended. The man gave an annoyed look but pretended to ignore it.

"Today should be fun but will also be extremely crucial," he said. "We are going to make a major step forward in spreading the Elkhart Ideal. This group will certainly be rewarded. 'What is our task today?' you may ask. Well, I'll tell you! Today we will be inciting civil unrest in low-income communities!

"By starting a riot we can hopefully perpetuate civil unrest in certain hostile areas at home and abroad. Today, we'll be starting in the United States, and other groups are working to continue pushing the civil wars in Africa. And we've got some fun ideas brewing for Europe and Asia as we speak.

"Here is our plan: Using our non-lethal nerve gas, we will be breaking into various law-enforcement agencies. We will disguise ourselves as police and SWAT members, and then we roam the communities and mercilessly beat various people. The ensuing outrage will lead to riots on a massive scale. We have operatives undercover in the field pushing certain rights groups towards violence and supplying them with weapons. If we are successful, we can get small scale civil wars started. Now for the details of action..."

The man's level of enthusiasm was beginning to get on Number 12's nerves. This would be the time he'd normally turn to Number 17 and whisper an off-the-cuff remark. He briefly thought of turning and making a remark to 57 but then pictured being shushed loudly. Number 57 was so uptight. So instead he sighed. He pushed it down into him and felt a slight sting in his chest. He thought about Sarah and the tone in her voice two nights before. He wondered why she hadn't answered her phone since. Or even bothered to return his calls. Then he felt another sting. He rubbed his chest a little. Someone behind him whispered: "Heartburn?"

"I dunno," 12 said. "Sure feels like it."

"Rolaid?" he asked.

"Sure," said 12, "thanks." He took one and swallowed it. He briefly wondered where the guy kept them, considering the suits they all had on, but decided it would be in his best interest to just let that one go. Don't ask. Don't tell. He managed to pick up enough information out of the briefing to know what he needed to do. Brutalize poor minorities all while impersonating officers of the law. A job's a job, he told himself. We all have bills. He still had an outstanding balance of over fifty-five grand on his loans, and it sure as shit wasn't going to pay itself. What the hell did he care anyway? Karl was dead. Sarah apparently hated him now. Who was left to give a shit about who he was? Certainly not him. Certainly not anymore.

24/ LAY-OFFS

"To show people what they have, you must take it all away."
–Damien Elkhart

Damien Elkhart had his finger in many pies. Elkhart Global Dynamics had hundreds of subsidiaries in dozens of industries. They owned companies that owned other companies. In fact, many people employed by Elkhart Global Dynamics didn't know who they really worked for. This was intentional for a number of reasons. First, because of the controversial nature of many of Elkhart's projects, any association with them would hurt potential business for the Elkhart-owned companies. Second, a key stage of Damien Elkhart's plan would have been hampered if the employees of the subsidiaries knew who employed them, or rather no longer employed them. Elkhart Global laid off millions of workers in all of their subsidiary businesses: construction workers, insurance salesmen, baristas, factory workers, and countless other professions ranging from careers to dead end jobs. This, in turn, would trigger a dive in consumer spending, leading to low profits for businesses not even owned by Elkhart. The result was economic turmoil. Communities in the third world that contained the sweatshops erupted in civil war. When this happened Elkhart himself sat in his high tower. He watched a thousand televisions beamed in worldwide. He unzipped his pants to subtly stroke his erection. He chuckled to himself and breathed heavily. With his free hand he mimed a conductor's baton as the choir of news reporters sang of "civil unrest," "economic turmoil," and "dark times."

He was showing everyone Truth. He was showing them what the world could turn into and what people truly were. Animals, pitiful and lost without his guidance. He knew it sometimes took horror for people to see Truth. And by God he gave it to them. The world began to spiral. The overture had ended. His symphony had only begun.

25/ KILL THE POOR

"Cleaning a toilet requires flushing it. So it is with society."
–Damien Elkhart

Number 12 stood outside the loading docks while he and his team were waiting for the trucks to transport them to the inner city. He lit a match by flicking it with his thumb, like he'd seen in the film *Double Indemnity*, and he lit a cigarette. He waved the match to put out the flame and took a drag.

"You shouldn't smoke," offered Number 57.

"Hmmm?" said Number 12, breathing out a stream of smoke. "Whassat?"

"Those things'll kill ya," 57 informed him, fanning away smoke that hadn't even been blown near him.

"Not fast enough," said Number 12.

The trucks pulled up and 12 flicked the cigarette away. It spun through the air and landed in a mud puddle. It went, "Psssst." The trucks squeaked to a stop and the gates in back opened as the ramp touched the concrete. The men filed in and took their seats on the benches along the sides. Number 12 sat down and strapped in.

"Remember," said the officer in charge, "when taking the station we must be as discreet as possible. We want people to think the police are perpetrating the acts we commit today. Understood?"

This was followed by a boisterous, "Yes, sir!" Number 12 looked around and he could see in the faces of the men that they were excited. Some had become believers. They would kill and die to live in Elkhart's world. Others wore more menacing grins, perhaps aroused by an excuse to act out their long-held racist aggressions. Number 12, however, felt nothing. Horror, guilt, excitement, and belief had all been robbed from him. He was so numb that even feeling numb no longer bothered him. This was where he was now and there was no longer any point wishing otherwise. He thought of his bills, the interest, and the crippling loan payments that left him with no choices. Even if there were other jobs, he certainly didn't have the time or money to find them. He was stuck. Simple as that. C'est-la-mother-fucking-vie. All these people were fucked anyway, he figured. What difference did all this really make? He felt the rocking of the truck. He closed his eyes and pictured all of the inconsequential lives they would take. He thought of all the inconsequential lives they would lose.

The truck pulled to a screeching halt behind the police station. Three men ran up to the door while the others filed out and into their designated positions. Number 23 came bounding down the middle with a device that looked like an adding machine attached to a cable with a card on the end of it. Number 23 slid the card into the locking mechanism on the door and punched in some codes. There was a slight "Ba-loop" noise and then he said, "Got it!" as he opened the door. The men in front held it part way open, and Number 23 trotted back whence he came. They looked at each other, slipped on their gas masks, and quietly did a three-count while signaling to everyone with their hands.

"I'ma club me some niggers," said Number 77 to himself and yet outloud. "Can't wait to club them fuckin' niggers."

"Three... two... one... Move! Move! Move!" The door swung open and several canisters of gas were fired into the building. Everyone ran in, shooting the canisters down hallways and into rooms. One cop was coming out of the bathroom just as they were clearing the hall. He took a canister to the face. It blew his head off. Within seconds the building was gassed and cleared.

The gas was a type of knock-out gas developed by Elkhart scientists. In solid and liquid forms, it was a powerful hallucinogen. In gas form it caused almost immediate unconsciousness, but the resulting nightmares it caused would be emotionally scarring. All of the unconscious bodies were stripped down and dragged into the back of a truck and piled on top of each other. Some of them were twitching and crying in their sleep as they were taken off to an undisclosed location. The dead body was dragged off in a bag, and the cleanup crew came through and quickly cleared the building of the still hanging gas.

The men suited up in police uniforms, and some threw on SWAT outfits. They took the police licensed weaponry. They were instructed to use only the weapons taken from the station so that bullets used on the crowds would be traced to the police.

"It won't do us much good if people recognize the weapons we're using and trace them back to us. Remember, we want this to be put on the law enforcement agencies," they'd been told in the briefing. Other units had taken out the neighboring precincts. Their target was a protest being held over the living conditions in the housing projects. There were also several plants that had shown up at the protest to help push it towards violence. The unrest stirred by the plants would provide the justification for the force used by "the police."

By the time all of the men arrived at the protest, the plants had already done an excellent job of rabble rousing. The recent wave of job loss had prompted massive civil unrest, and the mood of the protestors was increasingly tense and angry. The plants in the protest even carried signs that read "Kill the Fuzz." Number 12 stood in SWAT gear just behind the men with the riot shields, who stood by as the uniformed "officers" held back the crowd. One of the protestors (actually a plant) was being dragged away. The officers grabbed the "Kill the Fuzz" sign from him and beat him with it. Outraged, other protestor stepped in. The "police officer" drew a night stick and beat the interloper half to death. When others stepped forward, a "member" of the riot unit blasted them with a shotgun. That was the signal. The riot squad fired canisters of tear gas into the crowd.

Number 12 fired several rounds into the crowd. A man dove at him from the side. 12 extended his riot baton and swung it hard, bringing it right across the man's face. There was a wet cracking sound as the man's jaw was shattered. He hit the ground, his jaw hanging on by one hinge. The riot was spreading. A protestor drew out a gun and began firing back. Taking a cue, others began doing the same. Men in uniforms began grabbing and beating random passersby as well. The streets were filled with tear gas so thick no one could see. Occasionally through the gas there would be the glow of a car that was on fire. There was gunfire. There were screams. There was yelling. Number 72 had gotten his hands on a flame thrower and began forcing a crowd of people back into a corner. "Yeah!" he bellowed (though no one could really hear him), "Fucking niggers! Suck on that shit you fucks!" There was a burst of flame.

A man wearing makeup was sobbing. "Hey!" shouted 72. "Hey look! A flaming homo!" He blasted the man with fire, laughing, enjoying himself entirely too much. Number 12 didn't understand the people who enjoyed this job. Then again, he didn't find much joy in most things anyway. Can you lose your humanity if the world doesn't have any left? He just continued to swat away at people. He swatted away at flies.

Tear gas began to clear in his area, but the riots still spread throughout the city. Bombs began going off, and store fronts burst with glass. Number 12 took cover behind an overturned taxi. He took off his gas mask to catch fresh air. He looked around; the city had become a war zone. Actual police began to arrive and were attacked by rioters; they had no options but to fight savagely. The mission had been a success. Number 12 unzipped his vest and pulled out the pack of cigarettes that he'd been keeping there. He slid one out with his mouth and put the pack away. Surrounded by anarchy with a cigarette hanging from his lips, he felt around for a match or lighter. A flaming body fell next to him. He leaned forward, and taking a few short puffs, lit the cigarette. He took a long drag and sighed as bullets tore apart the street around him.

26/ PROMOTION

"What is faith without rewards?"
–Damien Elkhart

"Number 12 will please report to Damien Elkhart's office immediately."

Number 12 was on guard duty when the announcement came on. God's honest truth, he'd no idea why he'd been summoned to the office of their fearless leader. There was no certainty about it. But there were two distinct possibilities. It was either exceedingly good or extraordinarily bad. The guard next to 12 turned toward him. Number 12 couldn't remember the man's number. It was probably 50-something. It was hard to see his face with the visors down, but the smart money said he was shooting 12 an inquisitive look. 12 didn't give two shits regardless.

Number 12 made his way down the halls and through the elevators. He caught a tram that took him to the central offices. He gazed out the window of the tram as it came roaring out of the tunnels and he glanced upward. The building rose into the sky like the Tower of Babel. The tip of the tower had a lighted globe with an E on it. The company symbol that Number 12 had come to see so often he barely noticed. The tram was once again swallowed, this time into the bowels of the massive tower.

The recorded voices warned him in a half dozen languages to watch his step. He stepped off the tram and the doors slammed shut. Two guards checked his weapons, and the automatic door slid open with a "whish!" Number 12 was pointed in the direction of the elevators and was told he would have to switch elevators at the fifty-fifth floor in order to make his way all the way to the top.

After the long ride up, he found himself in the waiting room outside of Elkhart's office. There were many important-looking people dressed in everything from robes to turbans to suits. He walked over to the sexy receptionist.

"Yes?" she said.

"Number 12. I was told…"

"Yes. He's expecting you. Just have seat and we'll call you when we're ready for you."

Number 12 took a seat between a Cardinal and the governor of Texas. They sat in awkward silence as Muzak versions of Pink Floyd songs wafted in from the speakers in the ceiling. A poster on the wall featured an unfinished jigsaw puzzle and read, "Life is a puzzle. You are the final piece." When he saw a sign reading, "Every day is an opportuniDAY," Number 12 mouthed a vulgar expression.

"Number 12," the receptionist called quite some time later.

He stood and the Cardinal gave him a dirty look, presumably because he'd been waiting much longer.

"Wait long?" Damien Elkhart asked.

Number 12 had waited for two-and-a-half hours.

"No, sir."

"Good, good," Damien Elkhart said as he took a seat and motioned for Number 12 to do the same. Number 12 sat across the desk from Damien Elkhart.

"I understand you have done quite a few different things in your time here."

"Yeah. Guard duty, smash and grabs, excavations, chaos stirring…"

Elkhart nodded as he looked through files. "Yes, yes. I've heard. It says here you took out The Tank on your first assignment."

"Oh, uh yeah. Yeah I did."

"Impressive. He'd been quite a thorn in our side for some time."
Number 12 nodded.

"I've heard a lot of other good things as well. I can tell you and I have a very similar view on the world."

"Oh. Yeah?"

"Yes. Very much so. That is why I'm offering you a promotion."

"Really? To what?"

"How would you like to be part of our most elite units?"

"Why me?"

"Because you've shown you learn fast. Lately they've told me you've shown no emotions when it comes to work. You just do what needs to be done."

"I guess," Number 12 said.

"Don't be so modest. You've done stellar work. You really seem to be cut out for this. Only someone who believes in The Truth as I know it to be could dedicate themselves as you have. You've shown your only regard is for the spreading of the Truth."

"Does this position offer any sort of program to help pay off loans?"

"Let me put it this way... if you accept this position and excel at it to the extent I believe you are capable... you won't have to give a second thought to paying off anything."

Number 12 nodded. "Cool. Cool."

"Of course that wouldn't be your only reason for accepting this... honor. Would it?"

"What?" said 12. "I mean... of course not."

"Glad to hear it."

"Count me in," said Number 12, offering is hand.

Elkhart took it and shook it. "Your training starts immediately. Just head downstairs. They already know where to take you."

Number 12 stood up. "Oh. By the way, did I see some like... major religious officials out there?"

"Yes," said Damien. "They spent a large amount of money observing me and running tests for several weeks a number of years ago."

"Why?"

"Because of these things that I know to be true," he said.

"Oh," said Number 12, "of course. Thanks again for the opportunity," Number 12 told Damien what he wanted to hear. "I won't let you down."

"I know you won't," said Damien Elkhart. "Best of luck."

"Shelia," he said, pushing the intercom, "send in the Governor won't you?'

Number 12 stepped out of the office and was met by three men. "Come with us," they said as they escorted him to the elevator. "Congratulations on the promotion."

27/ ADMINISTERING EFFECTIVE TORTURE

"There's nothing you can do so well that I can't teach you to do it better."
–Damien Elkhart

Part of 12's promotion was attending a seminar. Number 12 sat at a hotel bar in a city people only went to if they had family or business conferences. He ordered a whiskey. He tapped the laminate on the end of the lanyard around his neck on the bar. "Rat-tat-tat. Rat-tat-tat."

He took a shot on the expense account and sighed. He tucked in his lips and nodded, then signaled the barkeep for another one.

His travel partner, a man from R&D, took a seat next to him. 12 had never met him before but had heard plenty. He was a poster child for creepy white guys. He had no official number that anyone knew of. Some called him Zero, or "Z." His job was hush, hush. When 12 asked him he just said, "Research."

"Hey, what are you drinking?" Z said. Number 12's travel partner was sketchy in a serial killer kind of way. 12 had been told his name but hadn't bothered with retaining it.

"Whiskey," Number 12 said.

"Too strong for me," Z said. "I'll just have a chardonnay.".

The bartender nodded and went to retrieve the wine.

"You got a little bit of red on you," said 12.

"Really?" Z said. "Where?"

On his own face Number 12 pointed on the left side, just where the neck and jaw line meet. Z dipped his cocktail napkin into the water and rubbed the spot and looked at it. There was some red on it. He looked back at 12, who pantomimed that there was a little more that he missed. He tried once more. Number 12 tilted his head a little bit to check again, then nodded. Z tossed the napkin to the wastebasket behind the bar. It was full of wet napkins and chewed cocktail straws.

Number 12 nursed his whiskey from the shot glass and was facing away from the bar, leaning back onto it. Z spun around and did the same.

A very sexy cocktail waitress walked by. She looked to be in her early thirties. Both men looked.

"Ow. I'd rape her with a power tool." Z nudged Number 12. Number 12 took a shot and ordered another.

12 drowned out Z's comments, continually checking his watch until he could finally say, "It's time to go." The two took their seats, which were just folding chairs in the ballroom. At the front of the room stood a stage and a giant screen with a screen saver of the operating system logo bouncing around. They picked up the yellow legal pads and ballpoint pens sporting the name of the hotel that had been waiting on the chairs. The crowd continued to pour into the room for a few more minutes. The ballroom was abuzz with people networking, playing catch up, and flirting. But in time the lights dimmed, the seats were filled and the crowd fell silent. A man walked to the podium to the sound of polite applause.

"Hello, everybody! And welcome to our annual Torture Symposium. This year we have representatives from a record seventy-five organizations, making this our largest one yet."

Applause.

"Today our keynote speaker will be Peter Meerza. Mr. Meerza is an expert on over a dozen methods of torture. He has worked as an interrogator for numerous dictatorships and has been a brain washer for numerous religious cults. Everyone, let's hear it for Peter Meerza!"

Applause.

Peter took the stage, and a PowerPoint presentation appeared on the screen.

"Thank you everybody. It's great to be here. A lot of people think their job is torture. And I guess so is mine."

Laughter.

"Today I will be talking to you about something I've been working on for a number of years. Maximizing the number of nails you can drive into the human head before death occurs..."

Peter Meerza clicked his remote and it moved to the next slide. What appeared was a diagram of the human head, not unlike an old phrenology model.

"What we have here is a diagram showing various places on the human head where a nail will not cause death but will still cause incredible pain. The key is to be very careful and really slow. Still, there are a number of variables that will come into play. Some people you will be working with are pretty thickheaded. At some point I'm sure you feel this way about everybody you work with."

More laughter.

"But the fact is there will be some people who are bigger, some people who can take more punishment than others. So first we'll talk about methods you can use on larger heads..."

Z jotted down notes. Number 12 began slumping in his chair. He dozed off for awhile.

"Keeping them steady is important. So you will want to strap the person down beforehand. They tend to toss around a lot when nails are being tapped carefully into their skulls. This can make precision excessively difficult..."

Time dragged on. 12 looked at Z, whose legal pad was filling up with verbatim notes and diagrams.

"Let me just warn you that this method can be dicey as a means of interrogation. Hit the wrong spot and you might wipe out any memory they have of what you need to know."

Laughter.

"After all, we are causing extreme amounts of brain damage. I find that this works best as a means of deterrent, punishment, or inquisition."

At this point in the lecture, a mangy-looking man was brought in by some guards. They sat him down into a chair not unlike one in a dentist's office, and strapped him down.

"Mr. Jefferson here was kind enough to offer his services today for our demonstration."

"Mr. Jefferson," as it happened, was a homeless man who had been offered fifty dollars for his "services."

Meerza held an electric shaver and began to shave Mr. Jefferson's head.

"You don't want any hair in the way, so begin by shaving the head." He lathered Mr. Jefferson's head and used a razor to make Mr. Jefferson bald. "Shave the head completely."

He opened a tool box and pulled out some very small nails and a tack hammer.

"Smaller nails, by which I mean thinner ones, will maximize the amount of space you have on the head. They are also more precise and keep the person from dying too soon." A hand was raised.

"Yes?"

"How many have you been able to do?"

"A little over two dozen. About twenty-five, twenty-six."

"Can we see it?"

"Yeah!" shouted someone else.

"I don't see why not," said the man running the symposium. "Let's hear it for Peter Meerza!"

Everyone applauded and then went quiet so Meerza could concentrate. They watched in awe. Number 12 turned to say something to Z but he happened to glance down and noticed that Z had developed an erection.

28/ TACO SALAD DAY

"You can take people out of the high school cafeteria..."
–Damien Elkhart

Thursday was Taco Salad Day in the Elkhart Global Dynamics cafeteria. Number 9 sat alone at the table she and Number 3 had claimed as their own. She couldn't help but shake those goddamned flashbacks of high school insecurity. No matter how time passes, you will always feel like an idiot sitting alone at lunch. Taco Salad Day was the day everyone would rush there early to secure a spot in line and assure deliciousness. Taco salad was the one thing the cafeteria could get right. Number 9, however, couldn't seem to do anything right. Her best friend was a traitor, and this fact brought about looks from others. Dirty looks, looks of pity, looks that questioned how she could have been so fucking stupid, so goddamn blind. Then there were the looks of suspicion. Maybe she knew the whole time. Maybe she was going to pull something herself. Maybe, just maybe, she knew and did nothing so she could passive-aggressively sabotage the whole operation. Whispered conversations were all about her.

She sat and ate her taco salad in silence. Every so often a whisper would tease her ear. But she would ignore it. It was equally possible it was in her head. She looked up and Number 12 had taken a seat across from her. She just looked at him. She had no idea what he wanted.

"How are you holding up?" he asked.

She just stared.

"I... uh... I got promoted," he said. "They sent me to a conference and everything."

She looked at him and then got up and left the table. She bussed her tray and left the cafeteria. He got up shortly after, cleared his tray with his food still on it, and stuck it on the belt that took it back to the dishwashers' room. He walked down the hall and took the elevator up to their usual rendezvous closet. He sprayed a touch of Binaca in his mouth and casually slipped into the closet.

It was empty. He felt around in the dark, clicked on the pull string lightbulb, and saw only a dust broom and an upside-down, dried-out mop bucket. He sighed. He clicked the light back off and decided to wait for a few minutes. After fifteen minutes he realized she probably wasn't coming. He wandered downstairs and stepped out on the loading dock to have a quick smoke. He hadn't eaten his lunch, and the nicotine would help suppress his appetite. He sucked the first one down very quickly and then dropped it into the smokeless ashtray that sat by the back entrance to the dock. He lit another and was halfway through it when someone poked their head out onto the dock. Number 12 had forgotten the man's number, having only met them the day before.

"Number 12," they said, poking their head out onto the dock. "Thought I'd find you out here. Come on up. Got one for you..."

29/ THE CAPITOL

"Don't talk to me of Big Pictures. I know the Big Picture."
—Damien Elkhart

After clocking out, many of the henchmen headed across the street to the Capitol Bar and Grill to take the edge off the day with draft beer and reasonably priced cheeseburgers.

The bartender polished glasses and eavesdropped on the conversations and philosophical musings of his clientele. He heard many stories and could even piece some of them together. He'd make the connections and put together the larger story. He didn't always hear it all and he never heard it in order. But he heard enough to know the score. More importantly, he knew enough to keep his mouth shut.

"They had to evacuate one of the underwater facilities this week," one patron was saying to another.

"I'd heard something about that. Completely destroyed wasn't it?"

"Yeah. I would know. I was there."

"What happened?"

"Don't know for sure. I was doing some work. Just standard lab stuff, y'know? The alarms started going off. Red lights flashing and all that. We heard gunfire and we didn't waste any time. I drew my side arm and ran for the escape pods. Number 133 saw one of the intruders and shot at him, but he was gunned down."

"How many were there?"

"Beats the fuck out of me, but I wasn't sticking around to find out. Whoever and however many there were, the place was set to blow. And I was the hell out of Dodge."

"So I was working the underwater facility," said a man on his fourth beer. "The alarm goes off and we all had our wetsuits on. But we're being told that the facility was intruded from the west submersible entrance. These fuckers want us to swim out and meet the douche bag! Can you believe that?"

"Wow. What'd you do?"

"What else could we do? We threw on masks and oxygen tanks, grabbed some harpoons, and went out to kick his ass. So we're swimming, right?"

"Yeah..."

"And this guy's got some special gun that can shoot underwater."

"I've heard of those."

"Yeah? Well he fires it at us and it just nicks this guy. I forget his number... 138, I think. Well, his arm starts bleeding and this shark gets a whiff of it right? This shark swims up to him and grabs him. Just starts shaking him. Fucking blood is everywhere. I mean everywhere. The water's all red. And so the guy fires at him again, and it hits the oxygen tank on his back and blows him and the shark up!"

"Holy fuck!"

"Damnedest thing I ever saw."

"Rough day?" the bartender asked a dejected-looking man with his arm in a sling.

"Rough week," he responded.

"What happened?"

"Broke my arm, got fired..."

"Here," said the bartender, pouring the man another drink, "on the house."

"Thanks."

"Why don't you tell me about it?"

"I was doing a maintenance job for Elkhart Global Dynamics at one of the underwater facilities. I was working down in the generator room. And this guy comes bursting into the room. I drew my handgun and shot at him. I missed. He got up close, grabbed my wrist, and broke it. My gun went sliding across the room. I went at the guy and he pushed me and I fell down into a lower part of the room. By the time I got back up, I was in severe pain. He was gone and he'd thrown the generators into overdrive. There was no way to reverse it. It was at critical mass. So I got the fuck out of there. I made it back to the surface. Company seen what went down on monitors, so they fired me. Something about not making more of an attempt to reverse the damage."

"Did you tell them there was nothing you could've done?"

"Of course I did!"

"Sorry. Stupid question."

"Next job I take is gonna be fucking union..."

"Good call. "

"Cheers," the man said, lifting his free drink.

"No problem." He noticed a man joining the group at table five. "I got to check on my tables." The bartender stepped out from behind the bar and headed over to table five.

"Tell Fred the story," said one of the guys.

"What's this story I've heard about?" asked the man who was apparently Fred.

"So earlier this week I'm guarding the escape pods at the underwater facility..."

30/ ELKHART MEADOWS

"Taking people into your arms justifies what was done to drive them there."
–Damien Elkhart

The henchmen and refugees walked along the avenue. The streets were littered with the remaining husks of cars. Smoldering mattresses had been dropped from the windows of the low-income housing complexes; their charred skeletal springs the only things that remained. The lingering remnants of tear gas stung the eyes of the men. A Humvee rolled slowly down the street in the middle of them. Behind the Humvee was a flatbed truck with a large double-sided screen. The screen displayed the visage of Damien Elkhart. He was speaking. He spoke of Truth, he spoke of evil, and he spoke of prophecy.

"Ladies and gentlemen. We are in hard times. But do not fret. I have foreseen these times. The challenges we face have come to me in dreams many nights for many years. But I have foreseen the solutions. I have been chosen to know these things I know and I will lead you all to our salvation. These men will guide you to the refugee camps. There you will wait for further notice.

"Ladies and gentlemen. We are in hard times. But do not fret..."

The people were led to refugee camps on the outskirts of the city. The riots started by 12 and his cohorts had rendered the city a war zone. Combined, the camps were only about half the size of the city that had been evacuated. There were some hastily constructed main structures. Really they were just frames and dry wall. The roofs were a thin aluminum, ruffled like a chip to give the rain someplace to flow. Additions to the building had been added on by the refugees themselves. Walls of the buildings were whatever they could find, including fallen billboards. The outside of one house was decorated with the tattered picture of a luxury sedan and proclaimed "0% APR!"

Numbers 62 and 12 led a group in through the gates, which were little more than a massive chain-link fence. As they entered the gates, they were given ration cards and housing assignments. They were then directed to where they could receive water, food, even cigarettes. Some booths were even recruiting people for jobs henching with Elkhart Global Dynamics.

As Number 12 sipped water from a faucet, he saw a group of young men sitting and leaning up against a "Best Network of the Year!" sign and noticed they were smoking weed. He approached them and stared. One boy looked up at him with defiance; the rest looked nervous. They had been busted. He snatched the joint away from the defiant boy and took a hit of it himself. He leaned against the wall and slumped down between two of the boys. He finally exhaled and passed it to the next boy.

He dozed. Sank into the wall. Fell slowly through an orange sky. The air had the viscosity of water. Though he lay on his back, he had the sensation of floating and looking down. He plummeted through a dimly lit tunnel. The walls of the tunnel, more a tube really, were built of rainbow colored dots. They looked like sprinkles. Looking over his shoulder he saw a strangely colored dragon or a demon in shades of purple, burgundy, maroon. He couldn't tell. Maybe shifting red to blue, blue to red. Perhaps it'd always been there in the layer of the world he could not see. This dragon, this demon, pursued him. Perhaps it always had. Or perhaps, equally likely, it had formed and grown only recently. One thing was for sure: It wasn't just weed.

Number 12 leaned against the spot on the board where the name of the "Best Network of the Year" had faded away. As his haze broke Number 62 walked over to him.

"Break's over, 12. They want us to bring in more refugees."

Number 12 nodded and passed the joint on. "Thanks," he said to the boys. He got up and headed towards the water reservoir with 62. They walked past a sign that read "Elkhart Meadows II."

Elkhart Meadows was the name given to the refugee camps set up by Elkhart Global Dynamics, a way of reminding the inhabitants to whom they owed this great debt of gratitude. Similar posters to those around headquarters were everywhere as well. "Triumph:," one poster read, "To Try with a Little Extra 'Umph!'" The visage of Damien Elkhart and quotes from his manifestos covered whole walls of buildings and light posts and even littered the streets.

The reservoirs at Elkhart Meadows were, in fact, a key component in the final stages of Elkhart's plan. The refugees, not surprisingly, were guinea pigs. The water was spiked with Capital T, a hallucinogen developed in the Elkhart labs. The people would be chock full of Truth when Damien arrived to greet them.

When Damien Elkhart arrived the people were feeling the effects and were wandering the camps in a daze. The people were herded by the henchmen into a large field just outside of camp. Groups numbering in the tens of thousands gathered in front of a stage and stretched out for over a mile. Trucks with screens were set up at various points, so those far away could see and hear the wonderful things to be shown.

31/ SECRETS

"Truth can never really be hidden."
–Damien Elkhart

Sarah's phone rang and identified the caller as T.K. She considered answering it but she just let it ring. She looked at it until it stopped. No message was left. Ron came in the door and his hair was wet. He was only half dressed and had bruises all over his body, as well as wounds that appeared to be burns. He collapsed on the ground.

"Ron!" She ran over to him and turned him over. He was shivering.

"S-Sa-Sarah," he sputtered. Thinking fast she went and got burn ointment. She put it on, and bandaged him up. She wrapped him in a blanket and went to boil some tea. So far she was avoiding the biting temptation to ask Ron what the hell had happened. She handed him a cup and sat down next to him.

"What the hell happened?" she asked.

"Sarah," he said, "I'm afraid I haven't been entirely honest with you."

Sarah held her breath. Her brother had come home like this before. She'd even patched T.K. up once or twice.

"I'm a member of a resistance movement called The Brotherhood Against Tyranny..." he said. Sarah jumped up and quickly moved away.

"That is so not fucking funny, Ron."

"I'm not joking. Look at me!"

"You... you fuck!"

"Sarah..."

"The B.A.T. killed my brother!" she shouted.

"What?"

"He worked for Elkhart Global Dynamics! You fuckers killed him while he was guarding an armory!"

"Sarah," he said, "I'm sorry. But if your brother was working for that evil son-of-a-bitch, than he was..."

"Shut the fuck up!" she yelled. "You don't know a fucking thing about

Karl!"

"I'm... sorry," he said. "Can I ask what battle he was killed in?"

"An assault on Armory-43," she told him. Ron looked confused.

"What?" she asked.

"We... uh..." he hesitated.

"We... uh..?" she mocked.

"We never made an assault on Armory-43..."

"What?" she said.

"We never attacked that building."

"Yeah. Right," she said. Her tone was clouded in doubt.

"I can prove it," he said. "You just have to trust me..."

"So..." she said, coming around, "what happened to you?"

"Oh this?" he said, wincing in pain now that he was no longer distracted from it. "I just blew up an underwater research lab..."

"Why?" she asked.

"It needed blowing up..." he said, lying down and rolling over.

"But... why?" she asked again.

Ron did not respond.

"Why, Ron?"

Ron had fallen asleep.

Sarah was sitting on the chair across from the couch when Ron woke up. She was smoking a cigarette and staring at him. Her previous attempts to quit had been spoiled by the recent emotional onslaughts.

"I didn't know you smoked," Ron said.

"We all have our secrets," she said. Ron said nothing. She tapped ashes into a small cereal bowl. "I want you to talk," she said.

"Yeah," Ron said, "we should probably talk."

"No," she said, "we don't have to talk. You've got shit to tell me."

"I'm an agent for The Brotherhood Against Tyranny."

"Yeah. That much you said already."

"We've been combating the corporation known as Elkhart Global Dynamics for a number of years. Its CEO and co-founder Damien Elkhart is a psychopath bent on world domination. We're out to stop him and others like him. Simple as that."

"Are there many like him?"

"You have no idea."

"Look. I know the types of things my brother was into, but we needed the money. It was just a job to him," Sarah argued.

"He still aided them! He is responsible for..." Sarah slapped him hard across the face. He looked back up at her.

"I'm sorry," he said. "I swear to you that The B.A.T. is not responsible for the assault on Armory-43."

"How do you know?"

"Because I'm one of their top agents," he said. "We are aware that the armory was assaulted. We know the M.O. matched ours. We've been looking into it."

"Why should I believe you?" she asked.

"The real question is what reason do I have to lie to you?" Ron said. Sarah nodded. "Fair point."

Ron touched her hand. "You know I wouldn't do anything to hurt you."

Sarah nodded again and squeezed his hand back. "I want in," she said.

"Pardon?"

"I want to join The B.A.T. My brother's life was taken while he was serving Elkhart. And he did it for me. I need answers."

"Are you sure about this?" Ron asked.

"For the sake of my brother and my own peace of mind, I've got shit to set straight," said Sarah. "Where do I sign?"

"We'll have to go to the headquarters," Ron said. He sat up and winced.

"You get some rest. We'll go tomorrow," she said.

"Sounds good," Ron said. "Help me to the bedroom?"

Sarah nodded to the couch, went to her room and locked the door. Ron saw the Tylenol PM on the coffee table. He took two, lay back down on the couch, and sighed.

32/ SOLVING PROBLEMS

"I've never done anything I'm not proud of. All of it will be justified."
–Damien Elkhart

Several days before the assault on Armory-43, a meeting was held by the highest of the higher ups. Damien Elkhart himself was in attendance for the briefing. So was the unit formerly known as The Dukes, led by Number 45. One of the head accountants presided over the meeting at the start. Number 9 was also in attendance.

"Gentlemen," said the accountant. Then after noticing Number 9 he added, "Ma'am. We are facing a major issue with the sales of some of our arms." He pulled down a chart featuring a line graph. The end slanted slightly downward.

"The issue is we're producing more guns than we are currently selling. We've flooded our own market and have had to drop prices on many of the weapons we've produced in the last year just to get them out of storage. Our supply is higher than our demand."

"I've heard enough about our problems," said Damien Elkhart. "What I'm more interested to hear is how we are going about fixing this issue."

"Well, sir... Lord... uh... that's why we called this meeting today. We were hoping to brainstorm some solutions..."

"The overproduced weapons," Damien interrupted, "where are they kept?"

"The majority of the product in question is stored in Armory 43, M'Lord."

"Destroy the stock," said Damien.

"Sir?... I mean... Lord?"

"Destroy the stock. Blow it up. We'll have less of it, we won't have enough to sell to everyone, and we can drive up the prices on what we have."

"How do you propose we do this? People will be wary to buy from us if we blow up our own stock. They'll catch on."

Damien Elkhart rubbed his eyes. "Then make it look like it was attacked by any number of our enemies. Must I think of everything?"

"No, M'lord. I mean... sorry, M'Lord. Very wise plan, M'Lord."

"I know it is! That is why I am the one to bring The Truth to the people! And if you ever question me again, I will have you cut open and fucked by rabid dogs! Do you understand me?!" His veins were bulging, his face red and sweaty. Number 9 handed him a pill, which he swallowed. He breathed deeply and sat back down.

"Very well," he said. "Here is the plan. Number 45, assemble your usual crew, and I will assign you a half dozen more. You will be briefed on the strategies of The Brotherhood Against Tyranny. You will all be tailored in the uniforms of The B.A.T. Posing as this group you will assault Armory-43. Kill guards if necessary, and it will be. The assault will take place in three days at 0100 hours. This meeting is adjourned."

Number 9's heart tightened. She knew Number 12 and his friend Number 17 would be on duty that night. She was flustered as she left the room.

Number 45 looked at himself in the mirror as he put on his leather trench coat. The coats and outfits had been taken from members of The B.A.T. who had been killed or captured (or captured then killed) over the years. The inside lining held all sorts of straps and compartments for weapons and ammunition. He and his crew had spent many of their waking hours the last few days watching video footage of The B.A.T. in action. They had practiced mimicking their M.O. and had complete confidence in their ability to fool their fellows. He checked his guns and clips one last time and then stepped out into the hall where his crew was waiting for him. He gave them all nods. They confirmed by nodding back. They headed out of the building and loaded into the van.

After the bomb went off, blowing a hole in an outside wall, Number 45 was the first in. Others laid down cover fire while he took out the guards. He ducked behind some crates of assault rifles while the ground around him was eaten at by bullets. He attached an explosive device to the crates and moved on, blindly firing to cover himself. A few bullets sailed through his coat, which he had intended to keep. So much for that idea. Fuckers.

He looked around and saw that some guards were putting up more of a fight than expected. A man had been blown in half. And as Number 45 looked up, he saw Number 69 get lit up with gunfire by a guard.

"Cooper!" he screamed. "Mutha fucker!" He fell to the ground just in time to avoid having his head taken off by gunfire. Debris flew about as grenades blew apart bodies and boxes. The alarms hollered. An announcement proclaimed the presence of active bombs and advised immediate evacuation. The guards ran out of the building. Number 45 dove out the back window and ran up the hill to the west of the compound. He checked his watch and then hit the detonator. He didn't get a very good look at the motherfucker who iced Cooper X. But he'd find out who it was and he'd fucking kill him. It was a promise.

Number 45 had obsessively reviewed the security footage from the assault on Armory-43. He checked the tapes from multiple cameras before, during, and after the attack and found the guy, no, the piece of shit who had killed Cooper. He now had the picture and began to seek him out. He scanned the picture into the employee records only to find he did not have the appropriate administrative access for the program. Multiple attempts kept bringing up the same error message. But Number 45 would not let this fuck over his revenge. He would have to try a different approach. Even if it meant showing the picture to everyone who worked for Elkhart Global Dynamics, he would find the son of a bitch. And he would kill him.

33/ THE B.A.T.

"Others will plot against me, which only proves that I am an agent of Truth."
–Damien Elkhart

Sarah Jenson began to work with the Brotherhood Against Tyranny alongside her lover Ron. She and Ron had tentatively patched things up after all the facts were in. The B.A.T., as it would happen, had someone on the inside that was privy to the information about the assault on Armory-43. Sarah sat at a table in a small room. Ron stood in the corner, his arms folded, not making eye contact with her nor she with him. Jonas Scott, a high-ranking B.A.T., plopped a file on the table in front of her.

The file contained a damning piece of evidence, a transcript of the meeting held by Damien Elkhart in which he ordered the destruction of Armory-43. Included in the file was a small audio tape recording of the meeting. Sarah placed the tape into a small player, put on the headphones, hit play, and listened intently. When her hand went up to her mouth, everyone in the room knew which part she was at. She hit 'stop,' removed the headphones and cried. Ron walked over to her and placed his hand on her shoulder. She reached up and touched it.

"Where do I sign up?" she said.

Sarah was shown down a hallway and taken into another room. Ron sat with her while Jonas left momentarily. Sarah sat in silence as they waited for Jonas to return. Ron opened his mouth to say something, but the words didn't come to him. A few moments passed before he tried again.

"You're doing the right thing," he said, then he decided to touch her hand. She nodded then sniffled.

After several minutes Jonas reentered with a cadre of men and women in black leather and sunglasses. They lined up behind him and looked forward, their hands tucked behind their backs. With a militaristic discipline they stood erect, staring forward and slightly up.

"You have expressed interest in joining the Brotherhood Against Tyranny. Consider this the point of no return. If you have any doubts, you should have expressed them twenty minutes ago." His dialogue sounded rehearsed, forced even. Sarah lit a cigarette. Jonas licked his fingers and leaned across the table, pinching out the cherry. "Being a member of the B.A.T. means rejecting the manipulations of corporate tyrants," he said. Sarah spit the cigarette onto the floor. Ron picked it up and tossed it into a waste bin in the back corner of the room.

"Do we understand each other?" Jonas said.

"Yes," said Sarah.

"Good. The Brotherhood Against Tyranny dedicates itself to the eradication of tyranny in all of its forms. We take the fight to those who wish to control us and those who attempt to oppress us. Wherever those with power keep those under them weak, we will be there. Wherever..." and he went on in such a fashion, his speech pattern paying homage to Winston Churchill but certainly falling short. It seemed to be working for the people standing behind him. Their chests swelled with pride as their leader rattled off their mission statement. Sarah could have sworn she even witnessed a single tear fall from the right eye of the man second from the left.

34/ MIRANDA

"Only trust those who've hit rock bottom. Only they know Truth."
—Damien Elkhart

T.K. headed out of his apartment and was getting out his keys when he was approached by two police officers.

"Tyler Kelly?" One of them asked.

"Yes?" he said, turning to them.

"You are under arrest for the kidnapping and attempted murder of the police officers of the fifteenth precinct."

Tyler just stood there and said nothing as they cuffed him and rattled off his rights. Another cop opened the trunk of his car, revealing a trunk full of illegal weapons that Tyler wasn't aware he had.

"You have the right to remain silent."

Tyler didn't struggle or speak.

"Anything you say can and will be used against you in a court of law!"

Tyler was as passive as he could be. This actually pissed off the cops more than resistance ever could have. They wanted an excuse to beat the shit out of him, and he wasn't giving them one. They tried to get a rise out of him. They handled him roughly, yelled, and called him names. Tyler still said nothing. He put up no fight. He just moved where they dragged him and kept his mouth shut.

Tyler made his one phone call to Sarah. She did not answer. He groaned and hung up. He did not get his quarter back. Tyler's court-appointed attorney was hung up with another case. If Tyler was surprised at the fact Elkhart Global Dynamics hadn't provided him with an attorney, he didn't show it. So he sat in the interrogation room while two detectives paced around in an obvious display of good cop, bad cop. They really did have it down. One offered him coffee. The other yelled. One spoke calmly and offered him deals. The other threatened him with phonebooks and called him foul, nasty names. He just stared. The "bad cop" became frustrated and struck him. Tyler's head was jerked slightly to the left. The cop was dragged out of the room, and Tyler just sat there.

When his lawyer finally arrived, he expressed outrage. The bargaining chip would prove too little, too late. The evidence against Tyler was abundant. His options were limited, and the lawyer advised Tyler to plead guilty. He hoped it would help lessen the sentence. Tyler went along but said as little as possible. The judge dropped the attempted murder changes down to assault and kidnapping. They apparently didn't know or care about the things that occurred during the riots. The police brutality while in interrogation shaved some time off his sentence and required the officers of the arresting precinct to attend a day-long sensitivity seminar.

When Tyler was called to the stand, he said nothing in his defense. The district attorney was a proverbial fountain of fire and brimstone, and his outrage was infectious. He was practically foaming at the mouth when examining Tyler, drenching him with spit in the process. Tyler didn't even wipe the spit from his face. He just stared at the spittle that would build up in the corners of the D.A.'s mouth. Tyler thought about Sarah. He wondered if she knew. He wondered if she cared. Tyler thought about Karl. The one guy he knew had his back was cremated and underground.

Who would feed his cat?

35/ HARD TIME

"Truth permits all. And this they always punish."
–Damien Elkhart

Tyler Kelly was escorted in handcuffs out of the courthouse. He stepped into the strobe lights of flashbulbs. His court-appointed attorney covered his face with his suit coat. He heard shouting. Questions.

"Mr. Kelly! Mr. Kelly!"

And.

"Tyler! Over here!"

He was stuffed hastily into the back of a cop car and was driven off to the holding cell at the station until he was to be shipped off to prison. Due to overcrowding and lack of funding, the state penitentiary did not have the facilities to hold him; he was to be sent to a privately owned prison. Tyler noticed the sign when walking in and let loose a slight grin when he noticed it was, "An Elkhart Global Dynamics Group." His sense of irony, it seemed, was still hanging on.

As he stood behind the line on the floor and signed in his possessions, he was being watched on camera by Damien Elkhart and Number 9. Number 9 smiled slightly as he removed his belt and placed it on the counter.

His pants began to sag and he held them up with one hand and finished signing the forms with the other. He slid the clipboard through the slot in the bulletproof glass. In exchange he was given a folded set of orange clothes. On the front was his prisoner number. On the back was the Elkhart Global Dynamics logo, the E over a globe. He changed into them only to find his pants were too big, the shirt too small. The pants barely hung onto his waist and his shirt stopped just above his belly button, giving the appearance that he was wearing a halter-top.

"Uh. Excuse me," he said. "Hey!"

The guard ignored him.

"These clothes don't fit."

The guard finally responded with a hint of resentment. "That's what we got. Just wear them for now and when we get them in your size, you can trade them out."

They escorted him to his cell, and hundreds of eyes watched him. Some lustfully. He glanced down at his tight-fitting half shirt.

"That's not going to help," he said to himself.

He was pushed into a cell, and they closed the door behind him.

"Back towards the cell door," the guard announced in a detached manner. Tyler did has he was told and his handcuffs were removed. His pants began to slip again and he tugged them up. He noticed his cellmate sitting on the edge of the bottom bunk. There was a small shelf along the left wall. It had a small mirror and roughly three dozen meticulously detailed clay figurines of kittens.

Tyler picked up one of the kittens, and his cellmate sat up.

"Keep ya' hands offa Muffin!" He blurted.

Tyler put Muffin back on the shelf.

"Sorry?" Tyler said.

" 'sokay," his cellmate said, "ya' didn' know. But don' let me catch you molestin' muh kittens 'gain." He walked over to the shelf, pushed Tyler aside without contempt, and checked on Muffin. Upon confirming Muffin's well being, he sighed. "Rugby." He said.

"Pardon?" Tyler said.

"Me name is 'Rugby.' Leas' dats what they be callin' me in 'ere."

"Tyler," Tyler said, offering his hand. Rugby shook it. His hands were callused.

Rugby was a big man. He looked to be in his late thirties. He had red hair with a touch of grey and a receding hairline. A scar ran along the right side of his cheekbone from his ear to his chin. Rugby glanced at Tyler's ill-fitting prison uniform.

"The hell they got ye wearing?" Tyler couldn't place Rugby's accent. It seemed to be a cross between Scottish and cockney.

"Man wear an outfit like that, his arse'll get tore the fouk up."

"The last thing I need is to be a sex toy. So don't even start that 'you got a pretty mouth' shit with me."

Rugby threw his head back and laughed. He gestured to nude pictures of ladies on the wall by his bunk.

"Believe me, lad. Ya got nuthin ta worry 'bout by me. Couldn't lock me away long enough."

"Oh," Tyler said. "Good."

"But serious, lad. Watch yer 'ole."

Tyler crawled up into the top bunk. He dozed off and woke up several hours later to the guards calling for, "Lights out."

36/ ...IN THE PAST...

"Time is not linear. It's more like a Spirograph.
Paths cross and it all goes around again."
–Damien Elkhart

As it would happen, Kenny D had spent time in the same prison as Tyler Kelly. He'd been picked up on possession with intent to sell. It was in his days as a runner, and the trunk of the car he was driving was loaded with too much to be a personal stash. And que sera sera, they booked him.

Kenny D wandered into the yard and, following the sage advice he was given by others who had done time, he walked up to the biggest guy in the yard and struck him across the right cheek. The biggest guy in the yard was Rugby. Rugby spat out a stream of blood. Rugby let out a belly laugh, and Kenny D put his guard back up, waiting for retaliation. Turned out Rugby couldn't have cared less. Everyone else knew Rugby well enough to know a fight was not going to happen. Rugby was capable of taking most people down. But Rugby never felt the need to prove it.

Guards rushed in and pulled Kenny D away and dragged him back to his cell. Rugby was checked out in the infirmary and returned to the yard when the doctors were done.

Kenny D stewed in his cell.

"Fuck," he muttered to himself. He'd cut the guy's face but the hit did not faze him. If anything he only humiliated himself.

The next day in the yard, Kenny D wandered over to a group of black prisoners. The ones who knew him greeted him warmly. They went into the gang's old handshake. Some of the others had seen his pathetic display the day before and smiled and nudged each other. Kenny D overheard them and his chest swelled.

"Fuck you, niggers!" he burst out and slugged one of them. "Fuck you!" he said again. He was pulled off by his cohorts before the guards noticed the disturbance. Among the circle any theories and jokes about

Kenny D being a pussy were quelled.

"We can't have you doing this shit," his old friend, DaMonte, explained. "We stick together in here, nigga, you know that."

"Yeah, yeah." he said, "Just tell them niggers to shut the fuck up."

"Hey, shut the fuck up, you niggers," DaMonte said to the others. Turning back to Kenny D, he said, "Feel better?"

Kenny shuffled his feet and shrugged at the man he'd pummeled, sending a mixed message of "Sorry" and "Say something, bitch." Then they shook hands, and the guy wiped the blood from his mouth and went back to weight lifting.

37/ THE SHOWERS

"Truth comes at the mind like a rapist.
It's often best to just lay back and take it."
—Damien Elkhart

Alas, poor Tyler, no one had passed unto him the words of wisdom given to Kenny D during his stay. He took no one out on the first day, or the second day. He was washing up in the showers after everyone had been to the gym. He was soaping up when he sensed somebody behind him.

"'Choo want, cherry?" a Zeus of a voice said. Tyler turned around.

"'Choo want a cock, boy?" The source of the thunderous come-ons was a man covered in tribal tattoos.

"Fuck off," Tyler said.

"Wha'choo say?"

"I said, 'Fuck off!'" Tyler said again, now noticing the stranger's raging erection.

"Naw, nigga. Youse muh bitch now." He backhanded Tyler and threw him to the ground. Some of the prisoners cheered the man on. No guards came.

The man forced Tyler back and forth.

"You best get used to dis, bitch!" He laughed. Tyler thrust his head back, smashing the man in the nose, shattering it. Blood sprayed out. Taking the opportunity, Tyler brought his knee into the man's exposed genitals. The man collapsed and Tyler smashed his face into the floor, then stomped between the man's legs until the guards finally came bursting in.

The other prisoners had backed away speechless. Tyler's assailant lay on the ground in the streams of steaming water with blood rushing from him. Tyler turned back to all the other onlookers.

"What?" he was spouting venom now. He walked right up to the guys who'd been cheering their friend on. "'Choo wan' some o' dis sweet ass?" Tyler mocked. They backed away. "Say something!" he screamed.

"Fuckin' say something!" The guards approached him, and as they escorted him away he spat some more blood at the inmates. They all backed away and then continued to wash.

When the guards returned Tyler to his cell, Rugby was carving a kitten out of a bar of soap he'd brought back with him. They did not look at each other. Tyler crawled into bed and lay on his back. He covered his face with his hands, elbows pointed towards the ceiling, small inches from touching it. He softly cried.

"I'm sorry," Rugby finally said.

Tyler rubbed his eyes with the thumb and pointer of his right hand and left out a huge sigh. "For?"

"I didn' t'ink it was yer first trip 'ere. I shoulda' given ye some words o' wisdom."

"What like... take a guy out the first day?"

"Somethin' like that. Best advice I kin give. Act like yer fouking nuts. People'll leave you th' fouck alone."

"I'll keep that in mind," Tyler muttered halfheartedly.

"'Ey, Lad. Lemme ask ye this. Ye see anyone fouk wit' me, ever?"

"No. But I only been here three days."

Rugby nodded. "True," he said. "Trus' me though. It ne'er 'appens."

Tyler nodded. "I'll keep that in mind."

"Ye' like this kitt'n?"

Tyler inspected it closely, "May I?" he asked, gesturing with his hands. Rubgy nodded and handed Tyler the soapy feline. The kitten was balled up in a napping pose. Its tail wrapped around it. The detail was stunning. Rugby had carved individual hairs along the back, giving the tchotchke an interesting texture.

"Don' be rubbin' it to 'ard," Rugby warned. "Is nah good fer th' soap."

"Sorry," said Tyler. He handed it back. "It's amazing."

"Thank ye'," Rugby said, adding it to the shelf. "I'll call ye'... Winkle." He rubbed its nose and lay down.

38/ EQUATIONS

"Slowly but surely all will see my light. My word is in electric crayon."
—Damien Elkhart

The reason 23 loved computers was because codes and mathematical equations always came out the same. When you knew what you were looking at, it was always predictable. He took to it for much of the same reasons and with almost the same fervor that he absorbed The Bible.

He believed so strongly in his job he even began to prefer his number to his name, Dylan Roffredo. However, his insistence that people outside of work refer to him as "Number 23" was usually meet with raised eyebrows and perplexed expressions.

"What?" his father said sharply.

"That's what they call me at work," Dylan argued.

"I don't care. I'm not calling my son 'Number 23.'"

"Why not, Dad?"

"Because it's asinine, that's why not."

Dylan's parents had nothing to do with his religious nature. They didn't bring him up that way at least. Dylan was always a timid child. He only felt safe with predictability, hence his love for math and codes and formulas. Dylan found God by means of a televangelist. The man was railing on about predestination, and Dylan liked this idea. Like a math equation, the solution was already there. It existed and there was no other answer it could possibly be. It was just a matter of solving the equation. So Dylan read The Bible and began going to church on Sundays.

His parents, who had always been quite liberal and existential people, didn't quite know what to make of this.

"What did we do wrong?" his mother asked.

"Don't worry, Hun," his father said. "It's just a phase. He'll outgrow it."

When Dylan got the offer from Elkhart Global Dynamics' internship program, he knew that it was where God wanted him to be. And though he did not always approve of his boss's methods, he knew there was a greater Truth behind it. He had faith that even though Elkhart Global did some shady things, it was ultimately all for the greater good. Elkhart was going to lead the world. He was destined to rule, to lead. Dylan could feel it. Dylan had already surpassed his internship time and was offered a permanent position, which he enthusiastically accepted despite opposition from his parents.

As Dylan's internship came to a close, he was approached by Number 122.

"Well, Number 23," he said, "it seems your time with us is drawing to a close."

Number 23 nodded sadly. In the last several months, he had truly grown to love and believe in what he was taking part. He'd grown to believe in Elkhart's preaching. They expanded upon his existing beliefs but still managed to change his perspective and shine new light on the Truth. He'd felt honored to be working with a man so full of the light of God, a man who spoke for God, and in a sense it was working directly for the creator and decider of all things.

"Number 23," said 122, "Damien Elkhart would like to have a word with you in person."

He couldn't believe it. Damien Elkhart wished to speak with him in person? In all his months there, he'd never spoken directly to Damien Elkhart and, other than the Drake Rodgers incident, had only ever seen him on screens and posters. What could he have done to receive such and honor? The walk down the hall, the ride up the elevator, even approaching the leggy receptionist all had about it a sense of pride and importance bordering on the surreal.

"Your number please," said the receptionist with the breathy, irritated voice of someone going through the motions.

"23," he said.

"Mr. Elkhart is expecting you," she said. "Please go right on in."

"You, uh, wanted to see me, Sir?" he said hesitantly. Immediately Dylan realized that "Sir" was not an adequate enough title.

"Sir, Dylan?" said Elkhart. "I thought you were a believer."

"I'm sorry, My Lord," Dylan corrected himself. He froze up in such disbelief. Damien Elkhart was addressing him by name.

"It's not easy," Damien said, "being the new Messiah."

It was only when Damien Elkhart cleared his throat that Dylan realized a response was expected.

"You do very well, M'Lord."

"Only with the help of believers such as yourself. Only with the help of..." he sighed, "believers."

"Thank you, M'Lord."

"But, I ask you this, Dylan. And I want you to think about it. Really think about it."

"I shall."

"Here I am, Dylan, imbued with the spirit of God, The Creator, The Great Author or what-have-you. I have been chosen because of these things that I know. But how can I spread this word if the people helping me spread it are not believers themselves?"

"With all due respect, My Lord, none of them are worth a damn."

"They do serve their purpose for now though, don't they?" Damien asked.

"Yes, Lord, I suppose they do."

"Which brings me to why I asked you up here today..."

"My Lord? Is my faith in question? Because I assure you I..."

"By no means," Damien Elkhart said, holding up his hand. "I assure you your faith is not in question. You're here as part of our internship program, correct?"

"Yes."

"And your time with us is almost up. Is that correct?"

"Yes," said Dylan, "sadly."

"Dylan, I'd like to offer you a permanent position. You fit our profile, you are a strong believer, and your computer skills are beyond anything expected. I need your help, Dylan. Do you understand? I want you to be there on the ground floor of the new world order. I want... no, need you to help me build My Kingdom in His Name."

Dylan merely fell to his knees and wept. He crawled to Damien Elkhart and kissed his feet and hands. Damien Elkhart just smiled.

39/ WINKLE

"'Insane' is the name small minds give to prophets."
—Damien Elkhart

"Act crazy," Rugby had said. "If'n people t'ink yer' foukin' nuts, nobody'll touch ye." Having beaten a prison rapist near to death, Tyler was already well on his way to following this advice. There was just one issue; the guy had friends.

Word was spreading around the yard that the man had bled to death in the infirmary. The other rumor spreading around was that he'd been patched up just fine but that losing the use of his cock had driven him to suicide. Everyone you asked would have told you something different about how. Some said he hanged himself with bedsheets, others that he slit his wrists, some said he stepped over the gun line, and others swore he drowned himself in the toilet. But everyone said he was dead and that his crew was looking for payback.

"Act crazy," Tyler thought as he was taken to the yard. His mind was abuzz with ideas on how he could act crazy enough to get people to leave him alone. He stood in the middle of the yard and noticed many of the inmates were staring at him. They'd heard what had happened and they knew who he was. Some hard-looking motherfuckers were leaning against the fence over by the bench press on the far side of the yard. Once they noticed him, they started in his direction. One patted the man on the bench press on the knee and motioned for him to join. He put the barbell back in place, sat up, rolled his shoulders, and cracked his neck. As they walked across the yard, their numbers grew. Guys joined from the basketball court, leaving the ball bouncing by itself before it stopped altogether and rolled away into the chain-link fence, rattling it ever so slightly.

Naturally such large movements of people don't pass unnoticed. Inmates saw men moving, they saw who was moving, and who they were moving toward. It didn't take a genius. A large inmate named Tyrone

(Tyler didn't know his name, of course) stepped forward and got right into Tyler's face. He was so close one would be hard pressed to slide a piece of paper between their noses.

"You in a lot of trouble, bitch nigga," Tyrone said, spraying spit as he spoke. Tyler said nothing.

"You know who the fuck I am?"

Tyler said nothing.

"Boy, I should fuck you up you don' say nuthin'!"

Tyler just tilted his head away from the flying specks of menthol mucus.

"You fucked my nigga's shit up real bad. Kilt 'em. You know that, faggot?" All his venom spewed forth with "faggot." Tyler, again, remained silent. This fact pissed off Tyrone far more than any smart-ass comment or bitter insult ever could. Tyrone grabbed Tyler by the shirt collar and threw him into the dirt. Tyrone picked him up again and slammed him into the fence.

"Say sumthin'! Say sumthin'!"

"Winkle is sleeping on the shelf with all the other kitties," Tyler said. It was the first thing that had come to mind. Its absurdity tickled him, so he giggled.

"The fuck?" Tyrone said.

"Meow," Tyler said.

"Crazy-ass motherfucker." Tyrone threw him to ground and kicked him. Tyler began to giggle. Others ran over and started whaling on him as well. Tyler howled with laughter.

"What you got to say now, mutha fucka?" Tyrone bellowed.

"Clip side of the pink-eyed flight?" Tyler said as he got up on his hands and knees then screamed with laughter. Tyrone kicked him in the stomach, and Tyler dropped to the ground, making a sound that sounded like a hybrid of sobbing and coughing. He rolled over and a huge smile was on his face. "Oh yeah!" he said. "Oh, yeeeah!"

Rugby stood in the corner, staying out of the ordeal. His arms were crossed and the guards rushed by him. Tyrone's eyes were about to bug out of his head, a vein in his forehead swelled. The blood-covered face mocked him. Just as he was about to swing again, a riot baton met the back of his head, then hooked him from under the armpits, and he was pulled to the ground. He struggled a little bit until he felt a needle stick into his neck. The last thing he saw before he blacked out was his crew being beaten into submission by an army of guards. More guards than he was aware of had been watching them.

Tyler was taken, again, to the infirmary. He'd been bruised up fairly bad. He had two cracked ribs, a broken nose, a scratched cornea, a split lip, and a good number of contusions and bruises. The scans had shown a mild concussion. So he was kept awake while lying in the infirmary and being treated for his wounds.

When he returned to his cell a few days later, he had on a temporary eyepatch, a cornucopia of other bandages, and braces.

"Damn, lad. They fouk'd ye' up som'tin' fierce," Rugby said. Rugby had been kind enough to move to the top bunk, having known full well that climbing up would have proven immensely difficult for his wounded roommate. Rugby was guilty of a number of things, but certainly not of being inconsiderate.

Tyler crawled into bed carefully, wincing as he brought up his leg.

"But truth be tol' 'm surprised they didn' break more on ye'," Rugby said. "Ye' one tough son o' a bitch."

"Thanks," Tyler said. "Means a lot coming from you."

"See, dough, they won' be bot'erin' ye fer a goo' long while. Most o' 'em were moved ta ano'er block. Tyrone was sent ta solitary for a few weeks."

"Who?"

"Tyrone. He was da' big one who started da whole t'ing."

"Ah," Tyler said.

"You'da been too if'n ye' hadn'a handled it way ya did."

"S'pose," said Tyler.

"No s'posing' 'bout it, lad. I know. Trus' me," Rugby said. There was a pause.

"What are you in for?" Tyler asked.

"Assault," Rugby said.

"That's all?"

"Ain't me first offense, lad," Rugby said.

"Oh," Tyler said.

"Too much o' th' creature. One too many bar fights."

"Creature?"

"Whiskey. Th' creature makes th' 'ead mean and th' fists quick."

"Yes. I suppose it does."

"Tha's why ye' can trus' me. All th' advice I gave ye' came from makin' de' mistakes meself firs'."

There was a brief moment of silence. Then Rugby said, "Ye' did good."

"Thanks for the bottom bunk."

"Anytoime, Lad. Anytoime..."

40/ PAROLE HEARING

"Be forewarned; I will test you."
–Damien Elkhart

The guard came to the door of Tyler Kelly's cell and callously banged his nightstick on the bars even though it was entirely unnecessary.

"Kelly! It's time for your meetin' with the warden!"

Tyler sat up and Rugby smiled at him. Tyler had been contacted by his lawyer the day before. He'd said something about a lid-blowing breakthrough in their defense case. Rugby stood up too. He took a look at Tyler and straightened his collar.

"Ye best be lookin' prim 'n' propa'," he said. Tyler's parole hearing had been in the works for a little over a week, and the time had come.

"Don' ferget 'bout ol Rubgy now," Rugby said.

"How could I possibly?" Tyler asked. The two men embraced and Rugby gave Tyler's ass a little squeeze in that totally hetero football player kind of way. Tyler walked over to the door and turned around; the guard cuffed him through the bars.

"Step away," the guard said. Tyler stepped away. "Opening door." The guard said. And the door opened. Tyler was marched down the aisles to the hearing room. Once there his handcuffs were removed, and he took a seat in a folding chair.

"Kelly, Tyler," said the Warden, who sat in the middle. The Warden was an older man but large. In his younger years he would have been in incredible shape. The remnants of his muscles remained, but their prime had since diminished.

Tyler stood up and nodded.

"Please remain seated throughout the hearing, Mr. Kelly."

"Oh," Tyler said. "Sorry." And he sat.

"Mr. Kelly, we are just waiting on..." Before the Warden finished his sentence, Damien Elkhart entered the room, followed by his usual entourage. Number 9 had looped her arm through his. He took a seat and she took her place behind him. "Oh. Mr. Elkhart. Good morning. We can begin now."

"My apologies," Elkhart said.

"It is quite alright, Mr. Elkhart."

"I was apologizing to Mr. Kelly." He gestured to Tyler.

"Oh... uh... don't mention it," Tyler said. "I had nowhere else to be." Everyone chuckled.

"Mr. Kelly," the Warden began, "your lawyer and Mr. Elkhart have brought certain developments to our attention. Certain developments that may very well absolve you of the accusations. Mr. Elkhart has also submitted video footage of various incidents of violent action on your part while incarcerated."

"I have monitored Mr. Kelly's stay personally for quite some time," Damien interrupted. "I personally feel that the actions on Mr. Kelly's part were in self-defense. I have submitted this footage to the District Attorney, who agrees these actions were clearly self-defense and that only the most ignorant of courts wouldn't consider it that way."

"Thank you, Mr. Elkhart," Tyler said.

Damien Elkhart turned to the Warden. "I have taken it upon myself, utilizing my own funds and resources, to further the investigation into Mr. Kelly's case. We were able to locate and arrest the guilty party. We also obtained a confession and the man is currently in police custody. Regrettably, this individual was within our own ranks."

"Oh, really?" the D.A. interrupted. "If all this is true then why did Mr. Kelly plead guilty in a court of law?"

"I'll field this one." Tyler's lawyer stepped in, looking to Damien Elkhart for permission. Damien nodded and his lawyer continued, "Due to the overwhelming, although circumstantial, evidence against my client, I entered a plea of guilty in hopes of lessening his sentence."

"But..." the D.A. protested.

Elkhart interrupted, "In light of this new evidence, Mr. Kelly is to be released immediately. Mr. Kelly will return to work for me. I will personally take responsibility for his actions."

"Well, Mr. Elkhart, I'm afraid the matter is..." the Warden began.

"Mr. Warden," said Elkhart with a piercing gaze, "I trust there will be no trouble."

"No, sir. None," the Warden said. The message was received. His strings had again been pulled by Elkhart. He might have very well done a little jig if Elkhart told him to. He was thankful that he didn't. But Elkhart snapped his fingers and a man came in with a briefcase. Its contents were all of the necessary papers and signatures to release Tyler Kelly.

Tyler signed his papers and watched as they stamped his file. He signed out the possessions he'd had. There was nothing of consequence: Shoes, a lighter, a wallet, and a watch that didn't work. His mother was waiting outside to pick him up.

"Hey, ma," he said.

She gave him a hug and they got in the car. Tyler didn't say much. His mother had a million questions that she wanted to ask, but she didn't want to hear any of the answers. So she remained silent for most of the drive.

"Honey?"

"Hmm?" he said.

"Oscar died," she said.

Tyler's head softly hit the cold window of the car, and he wept.

41/ BACK TO WORK

"Strength comes from doing what others won't. Only a strong will matters."
–Damien Elkhart

The Elkhart Global locker room was full of its usual buzz and noise. Strolling through, one would hear the usual, everyday stories of sexual conquest, as well as anecdotes involving things that would seem, in more conventional settings at least, quite disturbing. People boasting of head shots and whispers of how Number-whatever had fallen into some oddly placed machinery during a confrontation with one "hero" or another. When the door opened and Number 12 stepped in, the crowd held their tongues and looked up. Noticing the silence his entrance had inspired, he stopped momentarily.

"Morning," he said.

Guys came over, shook his hand, patted him on the back. One guy even hugged him. 12 responded with an awkward pat on the shoulder blade.

There were many different forms of "Welcome back!" thrown around. A few jokes about prison life. When someone made a crack about prison rape, he cringed and bit his lower lip. As he clenched his fist, the intercom ran the little monophonic ditty it played whenever an announcement was about to come on.

"Will Number 12 report to the main office? Number 12 to the main office."

He breathed out heavily, turned around, and pushed his way out the door. He took the tram, got on the elevator, and signed in at the desk.

"Mr. Elkhart wants to see you right away," the secretary said just as Number 12 was about to sit down.

"Oh," he said, "okay." He walked in and saw Damien Elkhart standing at the floor-to-ceiling windows and looking out at the city, in the distance were the lights of Elkhart Meadows. Number 9 stood in the corner. She showed no signs of recognition. Elkhart turned around to greet Number 12. He was smiling broadly.

"My boy," he said, stretching out his arms. "You have done me proud again."

"But I was thrown in jail," Number 12 said.

"Listen," Elkhart said, "I have a confession to make."

12 waited to hear what he had to say. Elkhart paused, intentionally adding dramatic effect to keep 12 stewing.

"I set the whole thing up," he finally said.

"What?"

"I was the one who had you arrested; I had a call placed to the police..."

"Why would you do that?"

"To test you," Damien explained in a calm voice. "I own the prison. I own the monitoring systems. I saw everything..."

"I can't believe this shit!"

"I got you out, didn't I?"

"But I actually was guilty!"

"So was the man who took your place. He failed me."

Number 12 said nothing.

"I'm sure it's hard for you to understand," Elkhart said, touching him on the shoulder. Number 12 swatted his hand away. "Listen, I was very impressed. You've proven your true potential. I want to offer you a leadership position. Effective immediately. You'd head up a whole unit."

Number 12 said nothing.

"You'll take the job, of course," Elkhart asked. He handed Number 12 a paper with a pay offer written on it.

"Yes," Number 12 said, "I'll take the job."

"Fantastic," Damien said, slapping his hands together and rubbing them. "Number 9 will show you where you'll be checking in from now on."

"Yeah. Okay. Great."

"Right this way, Mr. 12." She smiled. The first words she'd ever really said to him. As they went down the elevator, 12 wanted to say something but fought the temptation. The elevator doors opened and the hallway wound around. He was walking behind her and kept glancing down at her ass. Her cheeks moving up and down. He swallowed. As expected she lead him into a closet and began kissing him along the eyebrows then on the mouth. She brought his hand between her legs and guided his hand with hers until she was satisfied he had the rhythm right. She put her hand slowly into his pants and gently stroked and rubbed until he came. She wiped her hand off on his shirt and left the closet. He glanced at the cum-stain on his shirt. He licked his thumb and tried in vain to get the spots off.

"Here is where you'll be checking in everyday," she said as she led him into an office. "You'll pretty much just be doing what you've always done. The only difference is you're the one who will be calling the shots. You'll report here and get your mission assignments and your team a few days ahead of time. You'll have to review all of the intelligence reports prior to the briefings..."

Number 9 was really just going through the motions. She'd given this spiel so many times she could give it without putting much thought into it at all. Number 12 hadn't seemed as into it as he had in times past. The initiative he'd shown while in prison had really turned her on. His big promotion added to that as well. Maybe he was distracted by Damien's confession of the setup, or maybe the experiment was over. She would have to make more of an assessment next time if it ever came up again. Still, she'd needed some cheering up.

She'd had a dinner engagement with Damien Elkhart earlier that had thrown her off. She knew he did this for important meetings. She reached his office and he was standing by a table already set with salads. He gestured for her to sit and she did so.

"Katherine," he sat down. "I have something important to discuss with..."

"I'm Lucy," she said, confused.

"Of course," Damien said. "But that's what I want to discuss with you..."

"I'm not sure I understand."

"When Katherine left us, it left a void in both of us."

"Yes," she said, "it did."

He began breathing hard through his nose. Suddenly he picked up his knife and violently stabbed it into the table. He grabbed it again and stabbed the table repeatedly.

Lucy sat in silence. Stunned.

"Fuuuck!" he screamed. The knife stuck in the table. He instantly regained his composure and slicked his hair back. "It would not go too far to say that you owe me a favor or two, would it?"

"Damien, I owe you my life."

"Good," he said. "Good. Well, I was doing some research and I've found some things that may help with the cause. I need your help."

"Sure, Damien. Anything."

"Many of the world's enemies have a trait they share. Something they do that we don't. We must even that playing field."

"I'm listening..."

"Not only will it even the field for us against our enemies who do... it'll give us an edge over those who aren't willing to."

"What is it, Damien?" It always drove her nuts when he dragged things out for dramatic effect.

"I'm just trying to say that it occurred to me that to bring the world Truth we must resort to certain things. We must have the strength of will and in the end it will all be justified."

"What is it? Tell me!"

"We have to recruit children."

"What?" she said.

"Children. We'll adopt them, much like I adopted you. And we train them and we send them out to help spread Truth. I have a list of orphanages we can look at."

"Damien, I..."

He looked her in the eyes. "Your support means everything to me." He handed her the list. "Will you do this?

"I..."

He smiled then kissed her.

"I need you to get on this," he said. She was still stunned but apparently nodded.

"Great," he said.

She stepped out into the hallway, she stumbled over to a trash can, and she vomited. She looked at the paper, crumpled it up, and threw it into the can.

She rode the elevator down.

The ordeal had left a bad taste in her mouth. Washing it out with Number 12's spit helped a bit. Passive-aggressive behavior had been something that always rubbed her unpleasantly. Its prominence in certain areas of the company was growing. It was a form of manipulation she did not approve of. She'd always felt that the movement was about education, the stamping out of ignorance and the opening of minds. She still trusted it all as a whole, but she couldn't help questioning it. But wasn't a little doubt healthy? Sure. Sure it was, she thought. Of course it was. Still, something about the ordeal filled her with a Chekovian sadness. Though not knowing the expression, she'd probably put it some other way.

She looked up at Number 12, her distraction (one of them), and saw he'd been paying attention to what she'd been saying even though she hadn't.

"Do you have any questions?" She hoped he didn't.

He did not.

"Best of luck to you in your new position. And congratulations." She left the room. Number 12 looked as though he desired a kiss, yet he did not pursue one. She was both saddened and relieved he didn't. It was her own personal dichotomy. This was understandable, she thought. After all, human nature is paradoxical.

42/ CONFLICT OF INTERESTS

"One of life's great ironies is that 'natural urges' obscure Truth."
–Damien Elkhart

Ron offered to train Sarah. There was some dispute among the higher-ups in The B.A.T. Some argued that their relationship could very well cause a conflict of interest. It was also argued that their relationship would make the training process that much more efficient. Ideally Ron would already know Sarah intimately, how to communicate with her, and that would help her learn more quickly. The debate ultimately went in favor of those who felt the relationship would be beneficial to the training process.

He showed her how to fire guns, breaking and entering techniques, and various martial arts. She caught on fast but had much to learn. Ron recited to her the mission statements and explained the reasons The B.A.T. had taken it upon themselves to protect the interests of the world's people. She listened, she nodded, she asked questions.

Really she had come to doubt her relationship with Ron. But the idea of leaving had seemed too stressful, too dramatic. So she never did. Besides, he was always able to redeem himself just often enough. She came to the bittersweet realization that this was one of those moments. During a swordplay lesson Ron tenderly stood behind her and helped her with her trust. His chin hovered just above her shoulder, and their cheeks touched.

"Just like this," he whispered, getting a whiff of her hair, which was sweaty but still smelled nice. He noted this simply and directly. "How do you always smell so good?" She smiled and turned around. Tyler had once asked her that, and it almost bugged her that he wandered back in her mind uninvited. She and Ron kissed, embraced, slowly moved to the floor and made love. This caught the attention of a few passersby who peeked into the gym. They said nothing; just watched for a few moments before moving along.

Time passed in the manner of a film montage. Sarah had caught on in an impressive amount of time. In a few short months, she was ready for her first mission (It was no secret that The B.A.T. operatives were much better trained than Elkhart Global Dynamics henchmen).

Ron knocked on the door of her dorm. She had moved her things to The B.A.T. compound a few days into her training. "Hey, babe," he said, entering before she answered.

"Oh, hi," she said as she finished pulling her shirt over her head. She was a bit nervous. Not just because she was about to embark on her first mission for The B.A.T. but because taking on Elkhart meant a chance of running into Tyler. Not just running into him, but the possibility of running into him in battle. She kept her mouth shut on this topic. She wasn't even sure how much Ron knew about Tyler, and she didn't really wish to find out how The B.A.T. would react to her having a torrid history with someone in Elkhart. She was afraid they'd see it as another conflict of interests. She was even more afraid of them trying to find a way to use her relationship with Tyler to their advantage. That would have been the worst possibility. She walked with Ron down the hallway. They did not hold hands.

When they got to the briefing room, Jonas was standing by a large computer screen on the wall.

"Good," he said. "Now we can get started." He turned around and touched the screen, and a program came up. He quickly clicked his way around until he brought up a 3-D wire model of a building. "This'll be a good one for Sarah to warm up on," he said while still facing the screen. He spun around on the ball of his left foot and clicked his heels. "It's pretty basic," he said. "Smash and grab."

"Smash and..."

"Grab. Smash and grab," he interrupted her. "Elkhart's main source of income is weapons manufacturing. Of course they keep the best toys for themselves, giving their personal army a rather significant edge. We need to... even the score a bit." He rotated the 3-D model by touching the screen and dragging his finger around. "This is Armory-10. According to our intelligence reports, this is a storage facility for some of their latest toys." He proceeded to explain to her the route she would be taking through the building and highlighted guard posts with a touch of his finger.

Sarah nodded intently, occasionally nibbling at her pinky nail on her right hand. She nodded when she understood, asked questions when she did not. She would not go it alone; Ron and two others would be accompanying her on her first mission. She was thankful for this fact even if she no longer had feelings for Ron. But the fact remained he knew what he was doing; he was there for her and could guide her. She wondered, sometimes aloud, what else there was. Nothing came to mind.

Sarah was conflicted about the idea of taking lives but she wanted revenge for the death of her brother and she was beginning to entertain the idea of letting some of her morals slide.

43/ ARMORY–10

"All things are plotted by the Great Author."
–Damien Elkhart

Number 11 was milling around outside Armory-10. It was raining so he was wearing a poncho. The poncho was yellow plastic with the Elkhart Global Dynamics logo on the back and the word "Security" below it. With his body heat and the moisture of the rain, the inside of the plastic poncho was getting steamy. He moved to his 'B' position and looked up. He stuck out his tongue to catch rainwater to hydrate, if only slightly. It did the trick for the time being.

He was pissed it had come to this again. Standing outside in the rain was almost as bad as babysitting captives. Though, he had to admit, it was slightly less awkward. Standing in a small room, facing some prisoner, trying to keep a close watch and yet trying not to stare was the worst. His eyes would wander as he desperately tried not to make eye contact.

The rain picked up. The boots helped keep his feet dry but were uncomfortable. He shifted his feet a little and thought he felt a blister forming on the underside of his big toe and another one popping up under his heel. Dammit, he thought. The time came to shift back to position 'A'. As he walked his boots squeaked. He stomped his foot and shifted his weight in a vain attempt to stop the squeaking. It agitated his blister and he winced again.

"Damn," he said. "Nothing hurts more than a fucking blister," he muttered. A bullet tore through his calf muscle.

"Fuuuuck!" His cry drew the attention of other guards, all of whom were quickly dispatched by sniper fire.

"Was all that necessary?" Sarah asked Ron. "Did we have to kill those people? I mean..."

"Listen," Ron said with a stern tone looking directly at her, "those 'people' are scum, understand? They are parasites, okay? They make a living off the suffering of others and aid in the rise of tyranny. They are monsters, got it?" There was an intensity to him she had never seen before. There was anger and venom in his voice. He kept his intense stare until she nodded. A lump rose in her throat. He looked away and nodded to the others. He made hand signals and they made their move.

Number 11 was lying on the ground in a growing pool of water and his own blood. There was a corpse missing half its head laying inches from his face. Blood soaked into the mud, staining the ground. He coughed, and it hurt. It hurt a lot.

Sarah and Ron reached the fence, and Ron frisked Number 11 for security clearance devices. Sarah heard the body cough.

"Ron, I think he's still alive," she said.

"Finish him," Ron whispered as he hacked into the security lock. Sarah looked hesitant. Ron took note of this and said again, "Finish him. Do it!" His voice had that intensity again. It was vicious. She gasped sharply and put two bullets into Number 11's head.

"Got it," said Ron. His intensity had been replaced with a tone of pride and enthusiasm. He was about to, once again, fight the good fight. In they went. They ducked under an overhang of ruffled sheet metal. It caught and guided the rain away from the edge of the building. There, by the ground, was a duct just big enough for Sarah to fit into. Ron was too large and would enter elsewhere.

"You're not coming with me?" she asked.

"I can't fit. This is all you," he said.

"But, I thought you were coming with me," she protested.

"I have a different assignment," Ron told her.

"I wasn't told..."

"Need to know basis, baby," he said, giving her a soft kiss on the cheek. "Do your thing." And he was gone.

Number 12 was looking out the window in the security offices of Armory-10. His new job did pay better but he still took a few extra hours here and there. He was on a security guard substitute list and earlier that evening he got a phone call asking if he could fill in for the head of night shift security at Armory-10, who had come down with the flu. Number 12 said he'd be happy to. He crawled out of bed, having just nodded off, and glanced at his clock. He calculated that he could still get about three solid hours of sleep. He took a sip of coffee as Number 88 came in the door.

"Hooo-weee," he blurted out in a thick southern drawl. "It's really comin' down out there."

Number 12 concurred with a quiet nod and took another sip.

Night shifts weren't so bad. He'd worked plenty and was used to them. They ate into his social life, yes, but hell, what was left of that anyway? He scanned the security monitors, mostly moving his eyes but turning his head slightly when it was necessary. He had Thursday off this week so he figured all he had to do was get through this shift, a day shift, and another day shift and he'd be able to get a decent night's sleep. It wasn't too long to wait, all things considered. For an insomniac it was, to an extent, a moot point.

He knew enough to stay vigilant, so he poured himself another cup of coffee. He'd been on enough raids in his career to know that tonight was a good night for one. There wasn't much light and the rain fogged the world even more. He picked up a walkie-talkie off the console and checked in with Number 11.

There was no response.

"Number 11, check in."

Again, no response.

"Goddamn it," Number 12 mumbled and grabbed an assault rifle off the rack on the wall and a poncho off the hanger by the door. Number 88 took a cue and did the same, and the pair ran out the door.

"All units go to elevated alert," Number 12 told the walkie-talkie and all people on the other end. He hoped Number 11 had merely dozed off. Another guard would have come across him by now. That was, after all, a reason for pacing.

Now the only thoughts in his head were "Fuck, fuck, fuck..."

Sarah pulled herself through the vents. It was her job to sneak into the warehouse and unlock the storage room. Ron was to secure an escape route, and the others would be getting what they could of the weapons supply. She pulled a small notebook out of her pocket with the directions through the vents written down and double-checked herself. Two more lefts and a right. It was very cramped. There was no way in hell Ron or any of the other team members would have fit. She was the only real choice, but it didn't mean it was easy for her. She pulled herself a few more feet, and her cynical side told her this was the sole reason she'd been recruited. Her desire to curse was great but took a backseat to the importance of not making noise. From somewhere she heard gunfire and froze momentarily, then pressed on.

Number 12 had found the bodies. "Goddamn it!" he blurted out as he heaved his walkie-talkie against a nearby wall, sending its insides spilling. He grabbed the walkie-talkie from his compatriot and began barking orders into it. "We have confirmed men down. All units go to code red status. We are officially on high alert!" As he talked he walked toward a switch on the wall. Well, more of a button really. The button was under glass. Number 12 slammed the side of his fist through the glass, hitting the button. The alarm rang. His hand was cut slightly. He stepped into a guard station and took a bandage wrap out of the first aid kit and tended his minor wound. Everywhere red lights flashed and sirens wailed. Tyler reached into his pocket and pulled out a wood-tipped cigarillo. He lit it, and headed back inside the building. They were sure to be inside.

Ron heard the alarm sound, and considering he was standing right under one of the sirens, it startled him. He checked his watch. "Fuck," he said. It was much earlier than was anticipated. His obscenity was a bit louder than he intended and it caught the attention of a guard, who fired a round at Ron narrowly missing his head. Ron spun around and put two shots into the guard's forehead. These gunshots were heard by Sarah in the vents. They were also heard by Number 12, who quickly made his way in that direction. He saw a figure dressed in black and put a single shot through its throat. It coughed sputtered and fell to the ground. He pressed his back against a wall and ejected the round, the smoke from the cigarillo billowing out and wrapping around his head. Number 12 peeked around the corner and saw another figure in black searching the body of a guard, presumably for security pass cards. Having never actually seen Ron before, Number 12 did not recognize him. He stepped out and Ron caught him out of the corner of his eye, spun around and fired. The bullet hit the cigarillo, blowing it in half.

Number 12 ducked behind the wall again. He spit out the cigarillo. "That was my last one, you fuck!" he shouted.

Ron remained silent and quietly crept towards Number 12's position. Number 12 checked his belt and found he had not brought any explosive grenades with him. Just a few smoke bombs. He pulled one off his belt and tossed it around the corner. It landed directly in front of Ron and blasted smoke directly into his eyes.

"Aggggh!"

When Number 12 heard him cry out, he drew his knife and made his move. He dashed into the smoke, tackling Ron and pulled him to the ground, dropping his knife in the process. Ron began punching him in the ribs. Both dropped their guns. Number 12 pushed Ron away and swiped his legs out from under him. Ron fell to the ground, and Number 12 dove on top of him, striking him across the nose with his elbow. Blood sprayed forth and flowed down Ron's face. Ron saw a white flash, but he'd taken plenty of beatings before. He was trained for this shit dammit! He recovered quickly. He kneed Number 12 in the crotch. Number 12 fell back, coughing, and Ron crossed the back of his fist across Number 12's face. 12 spit out a tooth and staggered back, catching his equilibrium. Ron drew his knife and took a swing at Number 12 with it. 12 stepped aside, dodging it. He ducked the next swing and rolled to his own knife and scooped it up by the handle.

Ron was running out of time to make it to the rendezvous point. This asshole was really becoming a pain in the... well, in the ass. Ron ran toward the guns, but 12 moved quickly and threw his weight into his shoulder and his shoulder into Ron. Ron was smashed into a wall but pushed off of it, knocking Number 12 down. Number 12 kicked his feet and quickly pushed himself back up. Ron took a swipe at Number 12's torso with his knife. 12 hopped backward swinging his knife to block Ron's. The knives said "Ca-chink!" and spit sparks.

Sarah pulled the vent open and flipped down to the floor with the style and grace of a feather and landed just as softly. She quickly ducked behind a crate. Quietly prying open the box, she examined its contents and confirmed that this was, indeed, the private weapons cache of Elkhart Global Dynamics.

"Boo-ya," she said softly.

Ron slammed into 12. Shoving him back and back and back. He pushed him through a door, and they both stumbled down stairs and into the furnace room. Number 12 banged his head on a guard rail. He got back up and stumbled, felt dizzy, leaned over, and vomited from the concussion. Ron took full advantage of this opportunity.

He stood up but stayed low and charged at Number 12, grabbing his legs and flipping him over the rail down into the dangerous heat below. Ron gasped for air and limped back up the stairs.

Sarah checked her watch and saw she was ahead of herself, so she lay in wait. When the time came for her to open the door, she did so. Standing there was one of her teammates, but no Ron.

"Darren, where's Ron?" she asked.

"He ain't here yet?" Darren asked.

"No," she said.

"Well, let's take what we can carry. Hopefully he'll catch up. I'm sure he just got sidetracked with..." a bullet rudely interrupted him.

"Dammit!" he shouted. It had missed him but not by much. Darren fired at the source and the guard cried out "Ohhh!" as he fell from the balcony on which he stood. If the bullet didn't kill, him the wet "thud" of his head striking the ground certainly did. Darren took something out of his bag and unfolded a platform with wheels and lay it on the ground. He began loading cases on to it.

"Cover me!" he told Sarah. She fired her gun at their assailants. She didn't think she killed any, but if they were under cover they weren't firing at her. She had to duck herself when one attempted to blind fire. The guard took the opportunity to pop out and attack. At the end of a burst, she made a ballsy move and dove out. She managed to hit him twice. Head and chest. It was a good shot. It was mostly luck. All, really.

"Nice," Darren said. "Give me a hand." She helped him drag the load through the building, keeping an eye out for remaining guards; heads on swivels. Darren fired a few rounds into a guard rounding the corner. Sarah fired at a guard on the balcony, who in turn stumbled back with his finger still on the trigger and somehow accidentally shot one of his nearby comrades. It's funny how these things seem to happen.

"Dammit," she said, turning to Darren. "Where the fuck is Ron?"

Ron had reached the top of the stairs after vanquishing Number 12 in the furnace room. He opened the door and quickly made his way to an elevator. He pushed the call button and stepped in. He was smug, but still on his guard. He checked his watch and realized he was running behind but that he wasn't terribly late. He could still make it if he hurried; if this elevator hurried. He pushed the floor button a few more times; as if that would really help. "They really should have some express button on these things," he thought to himself.

The doors finally opened, and as he stepped out a knife was thrust into his heart, up through the chest from under the breast plate. Number 12 stared him right in the eyes.

"Sup?" said 12, watching the life flee from the eyes of his late-opponent.

Sarah and Darren reached the door, and Darren ran over to the keypad and plugged in his coding device. He managed to hack the door lock, and the door slid open. He didn't do it with the speed and efficiency that Ron could have, but that's why Darren was the backup, because he was capable enough. But he was certainly sweating the possibility that they had lost one of their top men on this mission. Darren was never made fully aware of the relationship between Sarah and Ron but he was perceptive enough to pick up on it without having to be told. With this in mind, he said nothing to her regarding it.

Sarah, however, was no fool. She was beginning to accept the tragic loss of Ron from the realm of the living as a distinct possibility. It would, for some time, cause her sleepless nights. Even when they returned to base, he had not joined them. The payload was less than they had hoped, but still The B.A.T. chalked up the mission as a successful one. They had lost a top agent, but the payload would help the cause. They would never say that he died in vain. When they rode into battle next time their arsenal would be even. Oh yes, Elkhart would be in for a surprise indeed.

Sarah knew her lover would never return. She accepted that with a level of grace and dignity that some would admire and others would dismiss as heartless. She had been on the fence in regards to their relationship in the weeks leading up to his untimely passing. That was for certain. Yet, she would never have wished for his death. His life had been too important; even if its importance in her own life was up for debate. She mourned him with the others. The unspoken consensus among The B.A.T. was, "What do we do now?"

The last full thought Ron ever had was, "How the fuck is that son of a bitch still alive?"

The truth is Number 12 managed to survive not because of his strength or because of his wits. He'd managed to survive because of an oversight on the part of Ron. After Ron had thrown Number 12 over the edge, he had failed to confirm his kill. Ten feet below the edge was a catwalk. At the end of that catwalk was an express elevator.

44/ THE GOOD SHIP PETROLEUM

"You are blind. Can't you see that?"
–Damien Elkhart

Number 9 knocked on the door of Number 12's office. He looked up from his desk, saw her, and cracked an awkward smile. He'd been going over his plans to scuttle the oil tanker one last time.

"Your team has assembled," she said then checked her clipboard. "Conference room 7b."

"Thank you, Number 9," he said. "I appreciate you informing me."

She smiled, patted the door frame, and walked off knowing full well Number 12 was staring at her ass. She felt sorry for him. Not for staring at her ass; he was more than welcome to do so. She knew he was living a lie. If he was fully aware of the things she knew, there was no way he'd be sitting in that office planning to risk his life, yet again, for the cause of Elkhart Global Dynamics. And though a part of her still deeply believed in the cause and the vision of Damien Elkhart, she was beginning to question the methods.

"Wake up, Lucy."

Those words cut into her brain. They were tattooed there. They went deep and caused an infection.

"Wake up, Lucy."

Number 3 was still impacting her life after all.

Number 12 entered Conference Room 7b and walked up to the board.

"Good morning, gentlemen," he said. Many of these men he had worked with before. Most of them were not "gentlemen" by any stretch of the most vivid imagination. Still, he followed the protocol he'd seen from the other side countless times before.

He explained the game plan, assigning very specific tasks to each man for very specific times. He informed them of the other unit that would be covering their escape. He told them where to be and when if they wanted to come back from this one. He said he assumed most of them wanted to. He was right, with only a couple of exceptions. (Numbers 77 and 109 were both suicidal).

Number 45 and his crew were going over their plans for the mission. But their meeting continued for a bit once all that had been covered. They were, of course, discussing the murder of Number 12 to avenge Cooper. They decided they would carry out their end of the mission as planned. Number 45 would be the one to find and cover A Team's escape. When doing this he would lead Number 12 the wrong way, fuck his shit up, and make full sure Number 12 suffered before dying. The Dukes would leave one boat for him, and he would escape after they'd left.

The meeting adjourned.

Number 12 was never much of a mariner. The up and down bouncing of the ship threw off his equilibrium. But he managed to keep his lunch down, which was more than could be said for 77, who was at that moment expelling half-digested food stuffs and various stomach fluids into the wake of the ship.

"Your man alright?" a crewman asked him.

"He'll be fine," Number 12 said. "He's just new."

"No sea legs yet, eh?" the crewman chuckled.

"More like no sea gut," 12 commented.

They both laughed.

"Well, we're glad to have you guys watching our backs," the crewman commented.

Number 12 and his men were posing as the Naval Reserves protecting the ship from potential attacks. The growing concern of piracy had made their charade that much more believable. Interestingly enough, many pirates, whether they knew it or not, were connected to Elkhart Global Dynamics in one way or another.

The crewman trotted off to do whatever his job was, and Number 12 heaved a sigh and prepared to do his. He walked over to Number 77, who was leaning over the side of the railing and spitting, and gave him a single rough pat on the back.

"All hands on the puke deck," 12 said.

"Oh, ha ha!" Number 77 said sarcastically, then spat again.

"Things are running on schedule," 12 told 77, "so we should be getting to our positions in the next half hour."

"Okay," Number 77 managed to say before expelling more of his breakfast over the boat's side. Number 12 unscrewed the cap from a bottle of water and took a sip before handing it to 77. 77 took it, wiped his mouth, and took a sip. "Thanks," he said, handing it back.

"You keep it," 12 said. Then he walked away.

Number 45 rode on a boat of questionable reliability. His crew consisted of his regular group as well as a handful of Somalian pirates they'd blended in with. They all dressed in dirty, torn clothes. No wonder they'd been assigned this job. They fit right in. Blow the ship, blame the pirates and offer to clean up the mess, save the day. It was Elkhart's usual M.O. 45 checked his watch; T-minus thirty minutes. At this rate it should time out just fine. That greasy motherfucker was somewhere on that thing. He'd find him and he'd get his ass.

Number 12 worked his way down to his position, glancing around all the while, confirming where the others were as well, and firing nods to the less proactive men to let them know now was the time. They took the signal and made their respective moves. Number 12 made his way to the oil. He wound his way between the massive tanks and came up behind a crewman. The crewman turned around and jumped back startled.

"Holy fuck!" he shouted. "You scared the shit out of me!"

Number 12 smiled and said, "Boo!" in a very quiet, non-threatening manner. The crewman laughed. Number 12 drew a silenced pistol. The man went quiet. Number 12 shot him in the head twice. The man died and voided his bowels.

"No kidding," Number 12 said. Such comments helped him distance himself, or at least they used to. Now they were more a force of habit. He began placing special non-incendiary explosives around. These would blow with a pressure hard enough to punch a hole in the side of the ship and oil tanks without blowing the whole ship to Hell in a ball of flames (at least not before they had a chance to get off). He checked his watch. The escape crafts would be leaving in five. He set the timers appropriately and quickly left. As he reached the top of the stairs, he heard the commotion on deck.

Number 45's craft pulled up alongside the oil tanker, and his crew began tossing the grappling hooks and climbing quickly up the side. Number 45 and the rest of the Elkhart members disguised as pirates began shooting crewmen left and right. Most of the actual pirates seemed very surprised by this sudden burst of violence but joined in nonetheless. The various Elkhart compatriots disguised as Naval Reserves ran to the boats, and Number 45 ran between them. He double-checked where 12 would be and made his way to the oil tank room. As he opened the door, the two nearly ran into each other.

"We gotta' keep moving," 12 said. "It's about ready to blow."

"Motherfucker!" Number 45 blurted out, aiming his gun right at 12.

"What the fuck?!" 12 shouted.

"You the fag that iced Coop!"

"What? Who the fuck is Coop? What the fuck are you doing?" 12 said.

Number 45 responded by cocking the gun.

Just then the charges blew, knocking both men down. Number 45 grabbed 12 and began whaling on him with a level of malevolence that would shock the most psychologically unstable heavyweight. Number 12 eventually grabbed both of 45's fists and headbutted him in the nose. Number 45 stumbled around and then managed to find his switchblade. He took a swing at 12, who jumped back and stumbled on the steps but still managed to dodge the temporarily blind Number 45. The base of the steps was filling up with oil. 12 paused, thinking about the next charge that was about to blow. He grabbed hold of the railings, leaving himself wide open. 45 took this opportunity to charge Number 12 and stuck his knife into Number 12's side. 12 grunted.

"Das right, muthafucka. Das right," Number 45 mocked. The charge blew, throwing 45 off balance again. 12 lifted himself up with the railings, swung and thrust his legs forward, kicking Number 45 down the stairs and into the oil.

"Fuck!" 45 shouted. "Motherfucker!" Number 45 stumbled out of the oil. "I'll kill you!"

Number 12 lit his Zippo and heaved it at 45's chest. Number 45 burst into flames and fell back, howling in pain and igniting the whole room. 12 ran for more than he was worth. He ran past the bodies and saw that one boat remained. He climbed in and dropped it into the water. He fired up the engine and rode off. He pulled the knife out of his side, tossed it into the water, and tended to his wound.

Who the fuck was Coop?

45/ THE DETOXIFICATION OF NUMBER 23

"Desiring Truth doesn't make you ready for it."
–Damien Elkhart

Number 23 had been a major player in one of the main bullet points in Damien Elkhart's plan. 23 had hacked into Public Works departments the world over. Elkhart's Truth drug had been introduced into the water supplies of dozens of major cities, and everywhere people were seeing the world hidden by their eyes. The line between the things they saw and what was really there had become thinner, almost transparent, and 23 could not be happier.

God guided his hands over sets of keyboards. God focused his eyes on multiple monitors and God made him wonder about this fantastic drug that showed people Truth. He, himself, had only had a little Truth in the early stages of development. And it was watered down, just like what people were getting out of their tap water. Dylan had worked too long, too hard, and was far too dedicated to see and experience only these watered down versions of Truth. Dylan wanted it pure, strong, and constant. And for the first time in his life, Dylan considered taking the initiative. He would go to the labs and consume pure Truth. He would have visions of the world and of God that few others could really see or understand. And when Damien Elkhart saw this initiative, he would take Dylan under his personal wing. Damien would tell Dylan all he needed to know and what he needed to think. Damien would interpret it all for him. The burden would be lifted. All of the burdens.

He sat up and made his way down to the lab. He walked to a window not unlike one at a pharmacy or doctor's office. The receptionist wore a lab coat and slid open the glass window.

"Yes?"

"I'm initiating a project and require a vial of pure Truth."

"ID?" she said. She was a heavy-set, middle-aged black woman. But Dylan was "colorblind" and took no notice of such things. He just handed her his ID. The woman examined the security clearance codes on Number 23's ID. She handed it back.

"Just a minute." She walked into the back. Number 23 knew he had clearance for it. He'd come a long way since being a lowly intern. The cause could not run without him, and he knew they saw that, just like he saw the otherworldly qualities of Damien Elkhart.

"Here you go." She handed him a vial containing 50 ml of pure Truth. "Sign this."

He signed the papers, thanked her, and made his way to a nearby washroom. He stepped into a stall, and there he unscrewed the cap and downed the vial in one motion. His eyes dilated and his muscles tightened. He squeezed the glass vile in his hand hard enough to break it, but he did not feel the shards being driven into the palm of his hand.

...

"Dylan?"...

Fingers snapped.

"Dyyyylaaaaan..."

Dylan was in a straightjacket in a padded cell. He was sitting in the corner. Straps held him to the wall. His eyes rolled around. A doctor stood in front of him.

"Aaaahhhh!" Dylan screamed. Though nobody knew at what.

The doctor was not startled by this. Not anymore.

"Dylan. Your parents are here."

Dylan saw no such thing. Dylan saw only Truth now.

"I'm not sure what to tell you, Mr. and Mrs. Roffredo," the doctor said with business-like compassion.

"How long will he be like this?" said one of his parents.

"Well, it's hard to say," the doctor explained. "The drug, whatever it is, has really overtaken him. We've been seeing a lot of this cropping up lately. There's actually an investigation right now about the possibility of contaminated water supplies."

"I've heard about that," said his father.

"But in those cases," the doctor continued, "it comes and goes. Dylan seems to have ingested a far more concentrated dose of it. I can't be sure how long it will take to leave his system or if it will at all. All we can do now is keep an eye on him."

Dylan hollered again. It upset his mother and she buried her face into her husband's shoulder.

"We understand," his father said.

Dylan struggled again.

"We should go," Dylan's father said. "His mother is really upset, and I should get her home." The doctor replied with a nod. As they left Dylan babbled in tongues, presumably about the things he was seeing.

He was no longer their son.

46/ PURE UNADULTERATED TRUTH

"Truth is a wrecking ball."
–Damien Elkhart

Number 12 sat at his desk, filling out an incident report. He wrote, in as much detail as he could, about the incident that had occurred between him and Number 45. He'd identified him by looking at the files regarding the escape crew on the oil tanker mission.

Elkhart Global Dynamics had swooped in to save the day by building a large rig at the site of the incident to help clean up and filter the waters. It made a great excuse to build another base and establish a stronghold in yet another corner of the world.

Number 9 paced around outside his office. She was having a major internal conflict about whether or not to enter, to tell Number 12 the truth he deserved to know. Not Damien's Truth, but the facts. The brutal, harsh, vindictive, painful, God-fucking-awful facts. She walked to the door and reached for the handle, and as she hesitated, Number 12 opened the door. He was surprised to see her.

"Yes?" he said. She pushed him inside, kissing his mouth, and he let her. Then she pushed away and walked around.

"I have something to tell you," she blurted. Her voice almost sounded whiny; her chest had tightened. She looked backed at him, threw up her arms and dropped them quickly. "Ohh. Fuck!" She said.

"Calm down." he said, "What is this about?" He tried to play it cool by pretending it didn't surprise him that she was speaking to him about something that wasn't related to business. But in his head it knocked him on his ass and through the floor.

"That," she said, gesturing to the report in his hand. "It's fucking about this!" She grabbed it from him and shook it.

"What about..."

"I know why 45 tried to kill you!" She was really worked up now. Number 12 said nothing. She looked at him and she was breathing hard. His jaw was slightly clenched and he was waiting for her to continue. "You..." she paused. This was killing her. "You killed one of his men. A friend of his from before they were ever hired."

"Huh?" he said, "What? When?"

She looked at him. Not certain she wanted to say, not certain he would really want to know.

"You have to understand," she began, trying to calm herself down. "What I'm about to tell you is going to upset you. It may even destroy you...'

He started to piece things together before she said it.

"Armory-45," she said.

He stared. His lower jaw quivered. A black hole was beginning to form in his chest. The acid in his stomach boiled and almost as a hiccup he said:

"What about Armory-45?"

"It... ," she hesitated for the last time, "it was an inside job."

Number 12 sank against a wall. "What?" he said venomously.

"Elkhart... Damien himself ordered our own people to attack Armory-45 and destroy large quantities of product. To make it look like an assault by the Brotherhood..."

"What... ?" he said.

"I'm sorry," she said.

His hands shook. He was fast becoming crimson. His skin, his mind, his vision were all red. His whole body began to shake.

"How long... have you known?" he croaked.

"I was there when the order was given..." she said. He came at her and slapped her, knocking her down.

"Why the fuck didn't you say anything?!" he screamed. She sobbed. Not for the slap itself but because she felt it was deserved.

"I... I couldn't..." she said.

"Jesus-Fucking-Christ!" he slammed his fist on the desk. She screamed, thinking he was going to strike her again. He grabbed the chair and smashed it around the room until he held two splintered legs. He shoved the computer on the floor, and it burst with sparks and smoke and glass and plastic.

She sobbed the whole time screaming, "I'm so sorry."

Number 12 collapsed. Tyler Kelly sobbed. Number 9 crawled over to him and held him. He held her too. His tears, snot, and drool were getting on her shoulder. She didn't care.

He hatefully kicked a piece of nearby debris. The intercom came on.

"Number 12," it said, "Damien Elkhart wishes your company."

Number 9 helped him stand. She dusted him off and wiped his face with her sleeve. Number 12 regained his composure. She put a hand tenderly behind his neck.

"You need to go," she told him. He nodded. "Are you going to be okay?" He shook his head. He was not looking at her. With her other hand she made him look at her.

"Look at me," she said. "Listen to me," she said.

He did both.

"You will be," she said. "I need you to. If you can't then I can't."

"Okay," he said softly. She kissed him on the eyebrow, the cheek, and finally on the mouth. He left to go speak with Elkhart.

"Don't do anything rash," she advised. He nodded.

When he reached the door, he turned and said, "I'm sorry I hit you..."

"It's okay," she said. "I deserved it."

"No," he said, "you didn't." He walked towards the elevator. She sat on the floor. She knew he had held back. Her cheek didn't hurt anyway.

Number 12 didn't so much push the button for the elevator as he punched it with the side of his fist. In the elevator he breathed heavily. He tried meditation techniques he'd seen on late-night infomercials on nights he couldn't sleep. It worked, a little.

The doors opened and he entered the waiting room of the office and walked right past the receptionist who got halfway through saying, "Hello Number 12, please go right in."

"You wanted to see me, sir?" he said to Damien Elkhart.

"Oh. Number 12... Tyler. Please come on in," Damien said.

Tyler looked at him askant.

"It's okay," Damien said, sitting down as finely dressed men brought in food, a delicious looking leg of lamb.

"Join me," Damien motioned. Tyler sat down and a plate was set down in front of him as well. "I feel," Damien continued, "that you and I should be closer."

"Excuse me?" Tyler said.

Damien laughed. "Not like that. I mean I've watched you and listened to you very closely. And I think you and I have the same views. The same vision of the world."

Tyler nodded, though he wasn't sure what it was exactly he was concurring with.

"I want to work more closely with you," he said. "I need a new partner in this. Together," he said munching on large bites, "we can really make a difference. Bring the world the Truth as we know it to be." The last part was kind of muffled since Damien was talking with his mouth full. He was increasingly excited. Then Tyler heard Damien gasp. Damien began choking on a piece of lamb. He sat up quickly. With every gasp the food wedged itself deeper in his pipe.

"Whhooowaa!" He grabbed his throat. "Whhhooowaaa!" He gasped again. His watery eyes looked to Tyler for help. Tyler grinned. Seeing this told Damien Elkhart help was not coming. He hit the buzzer, but no receptionist responded. His face was turning blue.

"I'd like to take this opportunity to file my notice of resignation."

Damien collapsed on the ground.

"You can mail my final check, motherfucker," Tyler said as he exited the office. Tyler passed the empty receptionist desk. In the hallway he passed her as she exited the restroom. He smiled at her and nodded. She smiled too.

As Tyler rode down the elevator, a desperate, emotional announcement was made.

"All employees of Elkhart Global Dynamics. Something terrible has happened. Damien Elkhart has been found dead in his office from apparent asphyxiation. All employees are to drop what they are doing and return home until further notice. I repeat. Damien Elkhart has been found dead in his office after choking on his lamb dinner..."

The voice was that of Number 9.

Damien Elkhart had educated many about his Truth but had not revealed it in its entirety to anybody. Whatever he had left to say went with him. He left no heir. His empire was ended by a lamb.

EPILOGUE

After making the announcement Lucy Morgan slumped into Damien Elkhart's office chair. His body was still on the floor. She waited for the buildings to clear out. She watched monitors of people walking home with perplexed expressions.

"What now?" silent lips moved.

When she was satisfied that the complex had been cleared, she pushed a button on the desk. A side table flipped over, revealing a control panel. She hoisted the body of Damien Elkhart over to it. She typed in a command for self-destruct.

"Please confirm identity. Damien Elkhart," the computer said over and over. She took Damien's hand and pressed it to the pad. "Identification confirmed. You have five minutes to vacate the premises."

She let the body drop and returned to the chair. With the building went the plans, the files, the labs, and the Truth Archives. The stakeholders could fight over what was left of the company.

And they would. Viciously.

She sat down at the desk. "You have two minutes..."

She rooted through the drawers of Damien's desk. There, on the top of a pile of papers in the upper left drawer, was a picture of Number 3. Of Kathy.

Lucy Morgan smiled.

Tyler Kelly stood in a hallway somewhere in The B.A.T. headquarters. "Glad to see you join the good fight," people said. "You will prove very useful to us," said others. "You won't be the first former Elkhart henchman to join us. But we've never had anyone who got as high up as you."

The crowd dispersed. And standing there was Sarah Jenson. For a moment all they could do was stare awkwardly. Tyler was almost ready to walk away when Sarah threw her arms around his neck. He hugged her around the waist.

"I'm sorry," she said. She kissed his cheek. He squeezed her a little harder to let her know she was forgiven. They broke apart and she wiped her eyes. He smiled.

"So..." she said, "we should probably get to the meeting."

He nodded. They walked in together. Jonas stood at a podium.

"Welcome, members new and old. Today the Brotherhood Against Tyranny can rest a little easier. But only for a short while. Damien Elkhart is dead."

A cheer went up from the crowd.

"Yes. Damien Elkhart is dead. And his poisonous teachings have died with him. At least most of them. And this is why we must remain vigilant. Some of his disciples remain. The company itself still exists, and its stakeholders will be battling amongst themselves for the reins..."

Jonas spoke on and on. Tyler was not paying attention. He looked at Sarah, who looked back at him. He took her hand. She squeezed back.

"Isn't that nice?" Liam Adams said softly to himself as he watched them from the ventilation duct. Then his attention drifted back to Jonas.

"It is time," Jonas said, "for us, the Brotherhood Against Tyranny to rise up. To protect the people of the world. To educate them. To show them what we know to be the path to the Truth..."

Kyle Decker is a graduate of Drake University where he ran the humor/satire magazine *DUIN*. He lives in Daegu, South Korea where he teaches English. *Cannon Fodder* is his first novel.

BLOG: kylecdecker.tumblr.com
EMAIL: kylecdecker@gmail.com

www.ingramcontent.com/pod-product-compliance
Lightning Source LLC
Chambersburg PA
CBHW030227180626
46810CB00008B/3009